"If...

Lucas said briskly, "everyone will still believe it's mine. Both our reputations will be damaged. And the baby's."

He took a deep breath. "So I have a solution. I'll get the baby I want, and you will, too. You won't have to worry about supporting it. And I won't have to worry about someone to take care of it."

He'd summed it up, but Susannah didn't look impressed.

"What solution?" she asked, facing him squarely, her chin up, ready to do battle.

Lucas swallowed hard, his throat suddenly dry. It wasn't easy to say the words he'd never thought to utter again.

His voice cracked with emotion. "Marry me."

When he stopped the truck at the streetlight, he

Dear Reader,

Silhouette welcomes popular author Judy Christenberry to the Romance line with a touching story that will enchant readers in every age group. In *The Nine-Month Bride*, a wealthy rancher who wants an heir and a prim librarian who wants a baby marry for convenience, but imminent parenthood makes them rethink their vows....

Next, Moyra Tarling delivers the emotionally riveting BUNDLES OF JOY tale of a mother-to-be who discovers that her child's father doesn't remember his own name—let alone the night they'd created their *Wedding Day Baby*. Karen Rose Smith's miniseries DO YOU TAKE THIS STRANGER? continues with *Love, Honor and a Pregnant Bride*, in which a jaded cowboy learns an unexpected lesson in love from an expectant beauty.

Part of our MEN! promotion, *Cowboy Dad* by Robin Nicholas features a deliciously handsome, duty-minded father aiming to win the heart of a woman who's sworn off cowboys. Award-winning Marie Ferrarella launches her latest miniseries, LIKE MOTHER, LIKE DAUGHTER, with *One Plus One Makes Marriage*. Though the math sounds easy, the road to "I do" takes some emotional twists and turns for this feisty heroine and the embittered man she loves. And Romance proudly introduces Patricia Seeley, one of Silhouette's WOMEN TO WATCH. A ransom note—for a cat!—sets the stage where *The Millionaire Meets His Match*.

Hope you enjoy this month's offerings!

Mary-Theresa Hussey
Senior Editor, Silhouette Romance

Please address questions and book requests to:
Silhouette Reader Service
U.S.: 3010 Walden Ave., P.O. Box 1325, Buffalo, NY 14269
Canadian: P.O. Box 609, Fort Erie, Ont. L2A 5X3

VIRGIN BRIDES

THE NINE-MONTH BRIDE

Judy Christenberry

Silhouette
ROMANCE™
Published by Silhouette Books
America's Publisher of Contemporary Romance

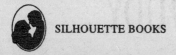 SILHOUETTE BOOKS

ISBN 0-373-19324-6

THE NINE-MONTH BRIDE

Copyright © 1998 by Judy Christenberry

This edition published by arrangement with Harlequin Books S.A.

® and TM are trademarks of Harlequin Books S.A., used under license. Trademarks indicated with ® are registered in the United States Patent and Trademark Office, the Canadian Trade Marks Office and in other countries.

Printed in U.S.A.

JUDY CHRISTENBERRY

has been writing romances for fifteen years because she loves happy endings as much as her readers. She loves traditional romances and is delighted to tell a story that brings those elements to the reader. Judy quit teaching French a year ago and devotes her time to writing. She hopes readers have as much fun reading her stories as she does writing them. She spends her spare time reading, watching her favorite sports teams and keeping track of her two daughters. Judy's a native Texan, living in Plano, a suburb of Dallas.

Dear Reader,

I never intended to marry again. My wife and child died, leaving me alone in my pain. But a man can refuse to live for only so long. And I have a duty to my father and grandfather. I need a son, someone to whom I can pass on my heritage, my ranch.

We may live a long way from the big city, but I've heard of surrogate mothers. You hire a woman, and the doctor takes care of everything. No emotions, no promises…no pain. Just a baby.

When Doc sent Susannah to me, I thought I'd hit pay dirt. I'd have my son, my future, without risking my heart. But when a woman is involved, things tend to get unpredictable. So now I'm in a heap of trouble.

These pesky women can drive a man straight to hell…or heaven. Guess I'm going to find out which way I'm going.

Keep your fingers crossed for me.

Lucas

Chapter One

"**W**hat's wrong with the old-fashioned way?"

Susannah Langston could feel the heat rise in her cheeks, but she kept her chin up. She was an intelligent woman, an educated woman. She wouldn't allow this...this scientific discussion to embarrass her.

"In case you didn't know, Doctor," she began crisply, "it takes two people to create a child the old-fashioned way."

The elderly medical man gave a rusty chuckle. "Well, I reckon they explained that in my first class. Not that I didn't already learn that lesson in the back seat of my—never mind." He cleared his throat. "Now, Miss Langston, I don't know where you came up with this crazy idea—"

"Doctor, artificial insemination isn't crazy, nor is it new."

"Hell, I know that. We've been doing it to the animals for years. But it seems a shame—"

"I'm sorry, but I'm not asking for your personal opinion," she said gently but firmly. "All I want to know is where do I have to go to have it—to get the procedure performed."

He leaned back in his chair and rubbed his chin. "You're all-fired set on this, aren't you?"

"Yes. My decision is not a whim. I've carefully thought out the complications, and I believe the reward will far outweigh the difficulties."

"You realize a pregnant woman without a man around will draw some talk even today? We're still a small community."

Susannah squared her shoulders. "If gossip becomes a problem, I can move to a new community after the birth of my child and pass myself off as a divorcée." In this day and time, single motherhood shouldn't carry a stigma, but she realized what should be and what was were sometimes two different things.

With a gusty sigh, the doctor leaned across the desk. "I believe I could do the job right here, Miss Langston. We don't have the capabilities of a major hospital, but, assuming you have a donor in mind, I could impregnate you with his sperm."

Damn! Susannah closed her eyes. Then her determination surged, and she stared at the doctor. "I don't have a—a donor. I assumed I'd go to a sperm bank."

She'd read articles in the magazines at work, in the library in Caliente, Colorado, where she spent her days. Sperm donors weren't in big supply in the library. Males weren't in big supply in the library. Only books. And dust.

The library was quite large for such a small town. It, and the money to hire her, had been a gift to the town from one of its late citizens who died with no heirs. Only books. Like her.

"Well, of course, that's how the normal person would go about it if we had a sperm bank. But we don't. And it'll be real expensive if you go into Denver."

She tried to hold his gaze, but there was a speculative look in his eyes that bothered her. "I've saved a lot of money."

"Hmm. If there was someone locally…"

He was staring beyond her shoulder now, his eyes almost glazed over in contemplation. Susannah wanted the interview to be over.

"Doctor, can you tell me the name of a group in Denver, or a hospital, where I can begin the process? That's really all I wanted. I want to go to the best facility for this…procedure." She should have done research and not bothered with this interview, but Abby, her best and dearest friend, had suggested Doc Grable.

"I think I know a donor," the doctor abruptly said, bringing his gaze back to her.

Susannah's eyes widened, and she blinked several times as she took in his bizarre statement. "What?"

"I think I know someone locally who would be a donor. And a damn good one, too. Good blood. Make you a fine baby."

"I don't think—"

"You go talk to him. I think he'll be willing. It'll help him, too."

"What do you mean?" Help him? How could donating sperm help a man? "I don't want someone from around here. It would cause all kinds of problems."

"None that I can see. And it would save you a bundle of money. Unless you've got more money than the city's payin' you, that has to be a concern. Having children these days, even the old-fashioned way, isn't cheap."

Susannah chewed on her bottom lip, a habit from her childhood she'd tried to rid herself of. Money was a concern, since she was alone in the world. But—

He shoved a piece of paper across the desk. Picking it up, she read a name and directions. Lucas Boyd. She didn't know the man, but she did know he had a large ranch in the area. Certainly he didn't visit the library. And she'd never seen him at church.

"Why?"

"Why what?" the doctor asked in return, his eyebrows rising.

"Why would this man want to—to be a donor?"

"I can't discuss why. That would be breaching a patient's confidentiality. All I can do is tell you to discuss your, ahem, needs with Lucas. What can it hurt? And it could save you a lot of money. Plus time."

"Time? I have two weeks' vacation coming. I thought that would be—"

"Lord have mercy. These things don't always take

right away. You're not going to the supermarket doing your weekly shopping, my dear. Sometimes it takes months.''

"Yes, but—''

"Go see Lucas. I'll tell him you're coming. Can you go right now?''

"Yes, but—no, I—well, all right, I suppose I could but—surely it would be better if I waited until you talked to him, gave him some time to think about what—'' Susannah had never felt more flustered in her life.

"Naw. Right now. I'll call and tell him you're on your way.'' He waited, watching her until she finally nodded.

"If Lucas won't solve your problem, then I'll draw up a list of the finest doctors in Denver. There are only a couple I'd trust with such a delicate matter, you know.'' He stood and came around the desk to pat her shoulder as she rose. "I'm glad you came to me with your problem, Miss Langston. One way or another, we'll take care of it.''

Suddenly she found herself on the other side of the door with it closed firmly behind her. She stared at the piece of paper. What had come over her? To agree to discuss such a personal thing with a stranger? To ask this—this stranger to be the father of her child?

The trembling that seized her almost took her legs from under her. She reached out for the wall.

"Are you all right, Miss Langston?'' the rosy cheeked nurse who'd worked for Dr. Grable for thirty years asked. She was a frequent visitor to the library.

"Yes, I'm fine," Susannah hurriedly said. "Miss Cone, do you know—know Lucas Boyd?"

"Well, a'course I do. He's lived here all his life. He's a good man."

Without meeting her gaze, Susannah smiled, hoping her lips didn't wobble on the ends as much as her knees were doing. "I—thanks. I'll see you later—at the library, I mean."

"Sure. I'll be in Saturday, as usual. Those last books you recommended were wonderful." With a big smile and a wave, she headed down the hall to another patient's room.

Susannah drew a deep breath and hurried from the office before someone else noticed her shakiness. She certainly didn't want to find herself back in the doctor's office.

Once she was behind the wheel of her car, she looked at the piece of paper the doctor had given her. It was damp and wrinkled, but she could still read the directions.

Directions to certain embarrassment.

She squared her shoulders. *You promised yourself you'd go through with your plan, no matter how embarrassing it might be.* And it would be embarrassing. But no more so than being the oldest living virgin in the entire state.

With a sigh, she started the car. Yes, she'd promised herself. She refused to continue to limit her life to rows and rows of books. Beloved books, but still only books.

She wanted more out of life. She wanted a child

to nourish, to shower with love. With whom she could be a family. Even if it meant embarrassment.

Lucas Boyd's housekeeper, Frankie, a cowboy injured by a bull a few years earlier who found riding more painful than sweeping floors, chased him down in one of the big barns beyond the house.

"Luke? You in here?"

"Yeah, Frankie. What's up?"

"The doc wants you to call him. Now. He said it's important."

Lucas patted the mare as he moved around her, his heart suddenly racing. "Did he say why?"

"Nope."

"Thanks, I'll be right there."

He stood still until he heard the slam of the door, signifying Frankie's return to the house. Drawing a deep breath to calm the excitement and fear that rushed through his veins, he began a slow, steady walk to the house.

Nothing to get excited about. Probably had nothing to do with the request he'd made when he visited Doc last week. Doc couldn't have found someone so fast, could he?

Hell, he'd been so unenthusiastic, Luke had figured he wouldn't hear from Doc at all. But Lucas had come to his decision logically. Three years was long enough to mourn his late wife, his beautiful Beth, and the tiny baby boy delivered stillborn.

Lucas knew he couldn't risk his heart again. That was too painful. But he needed a son to carry on the tradition of the family ranch. And to make the future worthwhile.

Doc Grable didn't agree with his decision to find a surrogate mother. The old geezer thought he had a right to interfere in Lucas's plans because he'd delivered him into this world. But it looked as though he'd changed his mind. Maybe Lucas owed him an apology.

Instead of using the phone in the kitchen, where Frankie could always be found, Lucas passed through to his office.

"Doc? It's Lucas Boyd. You wanted me to call?"

"Yep. I've sent one out to you. It's up to you, now. I still think it's a fool idea, but I've done what I can for you."

He wasn't going to have that argument again. "Thanks, Doc. When?"

"She should be on her way now, if she doesn't get cold feet. Name's Langston."

Before Lucas could ask for any more information, Doc's gravelly voice said, "Gotta go. Patients." Then the dial tone rang in Lucas's ears.

His hand was shaking when he hung up the phone. There was no going back now. He stood, then realized he wasn't prepared for a social visit. He smelled of the barn.

"Frankie!" he shouted as he rushed toward the stairs. "I'm hitting the shower. If—if I have a visitor, ask them to wait."

Because his future was right around the corner. And he didn't want to miss it.

* * *

"Luke, there's a lady to see you," Frankie shouted up the stairs.

A lady.

Lucas took one last look in the mirror, feeling foolish. He seldom studied himself, but it was important that he make a good impression on the lady downstairs.

After all, she was going to be the mother of his son.

Drawing a deep breath, he smoothed back his hair and then hustled down the stairs before nerves could get the best of him. Knowing Frankie would've put the visitor in the seldom-used living room, he paused on its threshold to take his first view of her.

She looked up as he appeared, then stood. Not a beauty, like his Beth. Her features were bland, and she was tall, lanky, almost. Somehow, those differences made what he was about to do easier. That, and the fact that he'd never seen her before.

"Mr. Boyd?"

"Yes, ma'am. Are you Mrs. Langston?"

"Miss Langston," she said, correcting him.

He frowned. In his mind, he'd assumed whoever agreed to his terms would be married, a mother already. From what he'd read, that was the typical profile. "You're not married?"

"No."

She added nothing to her blunt reply, but her gaze continued to meet his. He liked that. His son shouldn't have a timid mother.

Suddenly realizing they were both still standing,

he crossed the room and gestured toward the sofa behind her. "Please, be seated."

As she sat down, he noticed her skirt was long, hiding her legs. Probably has fat ankles, he speculated. Doesn't matter for a boy, he assured himself. Dark hair, like his. Beth had had pale blond hair, spun gold, an angelic halo. And a beautiful smile.

This lady wasn't smiling.

Of course not. Having a baby was serious business. He cleared his throat. "I assume you have no health problems."

She stiffened and then frowned. Dark brows rose and she tilted her head as she stared at him. "No. Do you?"

"None."

Tense silence fell, and Lucas tried to think of what he needed to say. "You understand that afterward...I mean, there'll be no contact between us?"

Her reaction was curious. A sigh of relief moved through her and a hopeful smile formed on her lips. Even that half smile made him reevaluate his impression of her. Her brown eyes warmed and a touch of color enlivened her pale cheeks. The severe style of her hair, pulled back into a bun low on her neck, didn't change, but she looked younger somehow.

"How old are you?"

She blinked several times. "Thirty-two. And you?"

"Thirty-three." He studied her. Yes, she looked that old. He might even have said a year or two older. "You're sure you're young enough?"

"I don't think that's any of your business," she replied, her jaw squaring.

One eyebrow slipped up in surprise as he stared at her. Not any of his business? She was going to have his son. "I want this...our agreement to be successful."

"My age is not a problem," she said firmly, looking away.

"Okay." He'd take her word for it since Doc had sent her. What would be the point of sending someone who couldn't have a baby? "Do you have any questions?"

"I—I know why I'm doing this, Mr. Boyd, but I don't understand...what are your reasons? Is compensation involved?" As she finished, she looked around the room, as if evaluating his worth.

"Didn't Doc explain the terms?"

She shook her head. "He said it would be a breach of confidentiality."

"Well, it's pretty simple. I want you to have my son, and I'm willing to pay." He leaned forward, his elbows on his knees, waiting for her response.

"*You'll* pay? But—but why?"

His eyes narrowed as he studied her. She was willing to go through the pregnancy gratis? Something wasn't right. Was she some kind of freak?

"I'd expect to. I'm asking a lot."

"I assure you, Mr. Boyd, payment isn't necessary on your part. I'm even willing to pay you." She raised her chin, as if expecting him to take her up on her offer.

He stood and shoved his hands into his back pockets. "Let me get this straight, Miss Langston. You're willing to get pregnant, have my son and then disappear, for free?"

"If you feel that my leaving the community is necessary, yes, I'm even willing to do that. The baby and I will find another home."

"You and the baby?" he gasped before responding to her in hardened tones. "The baby stays here, Miss Langston. We're agreed on that." He glared at her, wondering what her game was.

She rose, alarm on her face. "No, of course not, Mr. Boyd. The baby is mine."

"Damn it! What would be the point? I want my son! Why else would I go through the embarrassment of—"

"You thought I would give you the baby?" she demanded, her features tightening.

"Isn't that what a surrogate mother is? Someone who gives birth to the baby and then hands it over?"

"But you're supposed to be a sperm donor. Not a—you can't keep the baby."

"You think I would allow anyone, *anyone,*" he repeated for emphasis, "to take my child away? I've already lost one son. I'm not about to lose another one."

They were almost nose to nose now, his hands on his hips as he challenged her. She was even taller than he'd thought, only a few inches shorter than he was. Beth had been a petite doll, not even as high as his shoulders.

His visitor reached down behind her for the large shoulder bag she'd left on the sofa. "Clearly we have both—*I* have made a mistake. Dr. Grable suggested you as a sperm donor for my pregnancy. I apologize for wasting your time.''

''You mean you're not willing to be a surrogate mother?'' Lucas demanded.

''No.''

Again she didn't waste any words. As she moved to step around him, he caught her arm. ''I'm offering a lot of money.''

Tugging at his hold on her arm, she didn't meet his gaze. ''That's wonderful. Now, if you'll excuse me?''

''You're not interested?''

Her brown-eyed gaze flew to his eyes briefly before she stared at his hand clutching her arm. ''No.''

''You haven't even asked how much.''

Again she stared at him. ''Which should tell you I have no interest in your…intentions.''

''Then why did Doc send you?'' he demanded in frustration. From the moment he'd gotten Doc's message, he thought his problem had been solved. He'd almost imagined himself holding his child.

''You'll have to ask Dr. Grable that question, Mr. Boyd. I also have some questions for the good doctor.'' Her lips tightened, and he noticed their fullness for the first time.

Again she tugged at his hold, and this time he released her, stepping back, his cheeks flushing in embarrassment. ''You can name your terms, Miss Langston. I'll be generous.'' His jaw tightened as he waited for her to ask for some outrageous sum. But

he was so close to having his dream. He was willing
to pay.

Her response wasn't what he'd expected. Instead
of a calculating stare, he received a soft smile, gentle
almost, as she said, ''My dream is just as important
to me as yours is to you, Mr. Boyd. I can't do what
you're asking, for any amount of money. I'm sorry
I took up your time.''

Without waiting for an answer, she walked out of
the room, taking his dream with her.

Chapter Two

Someone had to bear the brunt of his anger, and it seemed only fair to Lucas that that someone be the doctor.

"Doc, what the hell game are you playing?" he demanded over the phone.

"Now, Luke, calm down. Did you talk to Miss Langston?"

"Yeah, I talked to her. But she wasn't willing to be a surrogate mother. She intended to keep the baby!" He couldn't have sounded more horror-stricken if he'd been talking about infanticide. "Why did you send her here?"

"It seems crazy, I know, but with both of you wanting a baby, I thought—hell, I'm sorry, Luke, but I don't like either of your choices. I was hoping to kind of jolt the two of you, if nothing else."

"Well, you succeeded. I've never had such an embarrassing conversation in my life. Who is the woman? I've never seen her before.''

"You might've seen her if you'd stop living like a hermit. You don't even come to church anymore, much less the few social occasions we have around here."

"Who is she?" he repeated, ignoring the other comments.

"She's the librarian...hired six months ago."

"Why doesn't she get pregnant the old-fashioned way?" If she'd done that, she wouldn't have raised his hopes and then dashed them to the floor.

"I asked her the same question. Seems she doesn't have any candidates around."

Lucas frowned. She wasn't a beauty, but she didn't put out any effort to attract the opposite sex with her concealing clothes, lack of makeup and severe hairstyle. But, hell, they were in Colorado. Single women, outside the big cities, were scarce.

"Why does she want a baby?"

"She didn't explain her reasons. All she wanted was information about how to go about it, not a discussion of why or why not." There was a pause and then Doc said, "You could ask her if you want to know."

"Has nothing to do with me!" Lucas snapped, irritated by the curiosity that filled him. "Find me a real surrogate mother, Doc. Okay? I'm ready to get this done."

"I'll do what I can. But you know it's not going to be easy. Or fast. That's why I thought—oh, well. I'll see what I can do."

* * *

"What are you reading?" Abby asked.

Susannah jumped as if someone threatened her very existence. With a protective arm over the article she'd been studying, she shrugged her shoulders. "Nothing much."

Abby McDougal, one of the volunteers who helped Susannah with the various chores of running the library, and her best friend, narrowed her gaze.

"You're working on getting pregnant, aren't you?"

"Abby, shh!" Her cheeks flooded with color as Susannah looked around to be sure no one had overheard Abby's remark.

"You are. I can tell."

"I'm reading an article. That's all."

"What's the title?"

"'Options.'"

"Aha! I knew it."

"So? I tried it your way. I spoke to Dr. Grable, but he told me I'd have to go to Denver for what I wanted." She fought to keep the blood from her cheeks because of the lie. After all, it was almost the truth. Without a local donor, she'd have to go to Denver.

She hadn't returned to Dr. Grable's office after the debacle of the interview with Lucas Boyd. She was no masochist. She figured she'd do the research herself. And she had. This article was the last she intended to read before she contacted a particular clinic in Denver. She already had the number written on a pad by her phone.

All she had to do was work up the nerve to make the call.

Heck, that would be a breeze compared to confronting that cowboy. That tall, sexy, handsome cowboy. Her emotions had gone on a roller-coaster ride that afternoon.

Exhilaration that her child would have this man for a father. Confusion when he told her he would keep the baby. Actually the son. She didn't think he had considered the possibility of a daughter.

Anger and disappointment when she realized he wouldn't cooperate. And forgiveness when she heard his admission of having lost a son. No one should have to suffer such pain.

Even though she'd been curious about his past, Susannah decided it would be best if she didn't ask anyone about Lucas Boyd. How could she explain her interest?

Instead, she concentrated on her desire to have a child. It would be easy to chalk up her decision to her internal clock. But she knew better. She didn't need a child for fulfillment. She loved her work and believed in the need to encourage reading.

But she wanted a child. A family. A way to pass on the important things she'd learned from her loving parents. A personal connection to the future. She actually ached with longing when she saw a young woman carrying a baby.

"Susannah, you need to find a man."

"It's not necessary these days, Abby. I can manage just fine without that added complication." She kept her voice calm, swallowing the tremor that ran through her.

Abby frowned. "Some man must've really done a number on you, Susannah. They're not all bad."

Turning her head away, Susannah tried to think of another subject that would engage Abby's interest. She didn't want to discuss her insignificant experience with men. The one time she'd thought she'd fallen in love, the man had dumped her because she hadn't accepted his advances with open arms. He'd labeled her frigid.

Susannah wondered if the newest shipment of books would distract Abby. "Did you see that we received the latest Nora Roberts romance? Have you put your name on the list to check it out?"

"I don't want to talk about books. What you're thinking of doing—"

"Morning, Abby, Miss Langston," a deep drawl interrupted.

Susannah almost passed out. She didn't have to turn around, or wait for Abby's greeting. That voice told her who was standing in front of her counter.

"Why, Lucas! I haven't seen you in a dog's age. What are you doing in the library?" Abby asked, a big smile on her face. "Have you met Susannah— well, I guess you have or you wouldn't have greeted her by name."

Susannah avoided looking at Abby, but she heard the curiosity—and speculation—in Abby's voice. "Hello, Mr. Boyd. Is there something in particular you're looking for?"

"Yes, Lucas, just what are you looking for? I've never seen you in the library before."

"Well, Abby, I'm looking for a private conversation with the librarian," Lucas said, a grin on his face.

Abby's interest sharpened. "Oh, really? Now, isn't that interesting?"

Susannah had no idea what the man wanted, but she knew she didn't want to deal with any more comments from Abby. "Could you please watch the counter while I talk with Mr. Boyd, Abby? I shouldn't be long."

"I'll be happy to."

Ignoring Abby's grin, Susannah looked at Lucas Boyd for the first time and drew a deep breath. The man oozed sex appeal. "Shall we go into my office, Mr. Boyd?"

He nodded and came around the end of the counter, then waited for her to lead the way.

Her back ramrod straight, Susannah stalked into her small office, wishing she'd cleaned her desk this morning. She wasn't compulsively neat, but she didn't want the man following her to think badly of her.

Almost laughing at that ridiculous thought, as if this man's opinion mattered, Susannah straightened her features and sat down behind her desk. She paused as he removed his hat and hung it on the antique hat stand. A shiver ran down her spine. The conversation must be important if he took off his hat.

"Won't you be seated?" she asked politely, gesturing to the small narrow chair across from her, the only other seat in the room.

He eyed the chair suspiciously, as if he didn't think it would hold him. He could be right. He was a big man, several inches over six feet, his body a solid mass of muscle.

"I think I'll stand. That seat doesn't look any too stable." He smiled but didn't wait for her response. Instead he turned away and looked out the small window. Since she knew the view encompassed the parking lot, a few scraggly buildings and the mountains in the distance, she didn't think it was that compelling.

"How may I help you, Mr.—" She broke off as she remembered their last meeting. Somehow her question seemed inappropriate. "I mean—why are you here?"

His intense blue eyes lightened slightly as he turned around, a grim smile on his face. Clearly he understood her change of question. "I think I owe you an apology."

He took her by surprise.

"I—I can't think of any reason."

"I can. I was angry when you—about the misunderstanding we both suffered two weeks ago. I don't think I was much of a gentleman about it."

She waved a hand in dismissal, but she couldn't trust herself to say anything.

"You see, I'd made a difficult decision. And I wanted to get on with it. When Doc said you were coming, I assumed he'd explained my offer and you'd accepted. I could already see my son—'' He broke off and turned back to the window.

Tense silence filled the room, and Susannah sought to ease it. "I guess an old-maid librarian was a bit of a shock, too."

He turned and stared at her attempt to smile.

"If you're an old maid in Colorado, it's got to be your choice, Miss Langston. We don't have all that many available ladies to choose from except in the cities."

Color filled her cheeks and she looked away. "I don't meet any men at the library."

"Why?"

"I guess they're not big readers."

He stood with his hands on his trim hips, watching her intensely. "No. I don't mean why don't you meet men. Why do you want a baby?"

She swallowed, her throat suddenly dry, then nibbled at her bottom lip. She wasn't about to bare her soul to this stranger. "Why do you?"

He frowned, as if surprised by her turning the tables. Well, she had as much right to ask questions as he did, she decided, raising her chin.

"For the obvious reasons."

"Me, too."

Frustration filled his handsome features. "That doesn't tell me anything!"

"But it's the answer you gave," she reminded him.

"Yeah, but I'm a—"

"A man?" She finished the sentence when he didn't continue.

A sideways grin only made him more attractive. "So I'm dealing with a feminist here, am I?"

To avoid looking at him, she picked up a pen and doodled on the pad of paper on her desk. "You're dealing with an educated woman, Mr. Boyd. Not one who's going to accept stereotypes and limitations because she's a woman."

He gave a disgruntled chuckle. "You're not like Beth at all."

"Beth?" She suspected the woman's identity, but she waited for him to confirm her thought.

"My wife. She—she and my son died in childbirth," he murmured, looking away. "Three years ago." He swallowed, as if forcing down emotion.

"I'm sorry. But no, I'm probably not like her."

"She was little...and sweet and beautiful." His voice was dreamy and sad. Then it changed as he added firmly, "And she always agreed with me."

"Well, that confirms it. I'm definitely not like Beth." She was ready to end the conversation. He didn't owe her an apology, and she didn't want to discuss beautiful women whose husbands adored them. Or little boys who died before they could even live. "I appreciate your apology," she said, rising, "but it wasn't necessary."

"Wait! I—you never explained why you want a baby."

"Neither did you," she said pointedly.

"I told you about Beth and the baby!" he returned. When she said nothing, he added, "I'm trying to work something out here!" He put his hands back on his hips, a scowl on his face.

"What?"

"Well, you see, there aren't—Doc hasn't been able to find a surrogate mother for me."

He looked at her, as if he expected a response, but she had nothing to say.

"I wondered if—I'll have to have someone take care of the baby when it's born."

Why would he tell her that...unless he thought she'd like the position? With a shrug of her shoulders, she said, "Yes, but I'm not looking for a job. You'll need to hire a nanny."

"Why? You could have the baby, and I'd hire you as the nanny. The baby would have the best care in the world, from his own mother." As if he'd finally made his case, he relaxed and smiled at her.

A beautiful smile. Too bad.

"And at night I would go home?"

"Yeah, I could handle things at night. After all, I'm his father."

"And the neighbors would think I'd had your child—probably as a result of a careless one-night stand—and I've given it up to you to raise, but I'm receiving payment to take care of it."

"I don't care what my neighbors think!" he growled.

"You may not, but what they think would harm your child. Do you care about him?"

"Of course I do!" he roared. "That's the reason we're in this mess in the first place!"

She moved from behind her desk, passing dangerously close to him, and reached the door.

"Don't open that door!" he rapped out, an order that he apparently assumed she would obey.

"Mr. Boyd, you are *visiting* my office. You do not give me orders." She opened the door. "Thank you for stopping by."

He stared at her as if she'd slapped him. Finally he took a step toward her. "You're not even going to consider my suggestion?"

"No, thank you."

"But we'd both get what we want."

"No, Mr. Boyd. You would get what you want. I would get crumbs, not even a piece of the cake. And I would lose my good standing in the community. Does that sound like I would get what I want?"

She could sense Abby's birdlike gaze flicking back and forth between them and wished she hadn't been so stubborn about opening the door.

He continued to glare at her, as if expecting her to explain herself further. Instead she stared at him, holding onto the door, hoping he didn't realize she might've fallen without its support. Finally, when she wasn't sure she could remain standing much longer, he smashed his cowboy hat on his head and strode from her office, not even responding to Abby's goodbye.

"What got stuck in his craw?" Abby asked, staring at her as she took her place behind the counter.

Susannah sighed, "I love you, Abby, but I'm not going to discuss what was said in there. It's private." She added a warm smile, which wasn't easy when she felt like crying.

Something must've alerted Abby to her fragile

condition. "Enough said. Why don't you go back in there and work on those orders. I can handle everything out here."

With a whispered thanks, Susannah fled into her office, closing the door behind her. She returned to her chair, where only moments ago Lucas Boyd had stood over her.

Great! Now he'd invaded her workplace. She already had trouble getting him out of her head from their one meeting. Seeing him as the father of her child had been a mistake.

As foolish as those thoughts were, she had dreamed of creating that child the old-fashioned way, as Dr. Grable had put it. Strange reaction from someone who was frigid. Those intense dreams had left her unsettled and wanting what she couldn't have.

Lucas's description of his wife, and the longing and love that filled his voice, had gouged a hole in her heart. Why hadn't she found a man to love her the way he'd loved his wife? Why was she alone?

And the biggest question of all: Why was it so difficult to have a child, so she *wouldn't* be alone? She'd faced the fact that part of her longing for a child was selfish. But she also knew that she would care for and love her child, provide for him or her, be a good mother.

Her child.

His son.

They couldn't be the same baby, in spite of his ingenious proposal.

It would never work.

* * *

It could work.

If only the woman wouldn't be so difficult. He was offering her what she wanted!

Her words replayed in Lucas's head. Well, almost. Couldn't she settle for what he wanted? The desire to hold his son in his arms was overpowering. He could see himself teaching the boy about the ranch, about his heritage. They would share the past and the future.

And Lucas would love him, his child, as he'd loved Beth and that other little baby boy. With all his heart.

He slung himself behind the wheel of his truck and drummed his fingers on the steering wheel. What now? Doc didn't seem to think he'd be able to find someone willing to have his baby.

The old man had suggested he go into Denver and find some poor woman who needed money desperately. Hell, he didn't want his child's mother to be a street person. She had to be strong, healthy, upstanding.

A dry chuckle surprised him. He couldn't say Miss Langston was weak. Or meek. Or agreeable. She was tall, too. He'd worried about his future sons with Beth. She was so little. What if—such a thought seemed like a betrayal of their love. But—

He turned the key and slammed the truck into Drive. He wasn't going to think about such things. Didn't matter anyway. Beth was dead. They wouldn't have children together.

When he stopped the truck at the streetlight, he

realized he was half a block from Doc's office. He'd make a detour and fill him in on the latest discussion with Miss Disagreeable Langston.

"You did what?" asked Doc, a comical look on his face, after Lucas revealed his conversation with the woman.

"I just told you. I offered—"

"I heard you. Lord'a'mercy, boy, don't you have any more sense than that?"

"What's the matter with what I offered? She'd get to have a baby, take care of it and get paid for the job, too."

Doc grinned. "And what was her answer?"

"She wouldn't even consider it."

"That doesn't surprise me."

"So why did you suggest such a disagreeable woman?"

"Disagreeable? Susannah Langston? Everyone loves her. She's patient with the elderly, gentle and loving with the children and extremely knowledgeable about her job. What's not to like?"

"She wasn't gentle, loving or patient with me."

"And were you any of those with her?"

"Hell, no! I just met the woman."

"Then why expect anything different in return?"

"You're turning the tables on me, just like she did," Lucas complained, frowning fiercely. What was wrong with everyone today?

"Lucas, you're spoiled. You've been running a huge operation for about eight years now, and everyone jumps to your command. Your wife was a sweet lady, beautiful, but she would've jumped off a bridge if you told her to. When was the last time someone told you no?''

"Today," he replied grimly.

"Exactly, and you're upset that she didn't see everything your way."

Lucas sprang from his chair and paced the office. "Okay, okay, maybe it isn't the best deal for her. But—but I need my son, Doc," he whispered, his head bowed. "I need a reason to keep going, to look to the future."

Dr. Grable stood and came around the desk to put an arm around Lucas's shoulders. "I know you do, son. And I'm going to help you."

Chapter Three

"How?" Lucas asked hoarsely. He hadn't intended to break down in front of Doc—or anyone for that matter. He was embarrassed and anxious to get back in control.

"It's simple. You marry the woman."

He stared at the old man. Doc must've lost his mind. "I can't do that, Doc, and you know it!"

"'Course you can."

He jerked away from Doc's touch. "No, I can't. I can't let myself—I loved Beth!"

"I know you did, son. But that doesn't mean you can't marry again. Lots of men do." Doc moved back to his chair. "Come sit down and let's talk about it."

"No! When I lost Beth and my baby boy, I vowed I'd never—I can't do that, Doc!" He clenched his jaw. A man didn't cry, especially not where someone else could see him.

"You took a few hits that year," Doc said calmly. "After all, your father had been dead only a few months. And your friend Billy died in that car crash in Denver. A rough time."

Lucas shook his head and stared out the window. He'd been doing a lot of that lately. But it was easier than facing Doc's pity.

"But that doesn't matter, because I'm not asking you to love Miss Langston. Just to marry her."

Lucas turned to stare at Doc. If he'd thought him crazy before, now he knew it. "Come on, Doc. She wouldn't even consider what I offered today. If I tried that idea on her, she'd slug me."

"Why?"

"*Why?* No woman would consider that kind of marriage proposal! It's an insult."

"It's my belief there are a lot more marriages based on practical reasons than there are based on love. And if you look at it from a practical angle, it meets all of your and her requirements."

"I don't see how," Lucas said, but he took the chair in front of Doc's desk, listening intently.

Doc raised his hand and began counting off his reasons. "You get your son *and* someone to take care of him. And no gossip. She gets her baby and someone to support both of them. And no gossip."

Put that way, Doc's idea seemed simple. But Lucas didn't think a female would think the same way. "I don't believe Miss Langston would agree with you. In fact, I'm sure she wouldn't. She hasn't agreed with anything *I've* said!"

"Maybe you haven't approached her right. You gotta give her a little romance, take her out to din—"

Before he could finish, Lucas jumped up from his chair. "Wait a minute! You said no romance!"

"Nope. I said no love. Women set a lot of store by romance. You know the things—flowers, gifts... All that takes is a little money and a little thinking."

"I'm not going to mislead her," Lucas muttered as he stared at the calendar on Doc's desk. He didn't realize his mistake until he looked at Doc and discovered a big grin on his face. "I haven't agreed to it!" he hurriedly said.

"Just think about it, son. Just think about it."

Susannah pulled herself together after a few minutes. It was foolish to wish for what she couldn't have. She'd learned that lesson a long time ago when the petite, pretty blondes, girls like Beth Boyd, took the roles of cheerleaders, homecoming queens and popular dates, while the tall, gawky, plain girls sat home, waiting for the phone to ring.

It was no surprise that Lucas Boyd still loved his dead wife. And mourned his baby boy. His pain had touched her again. She could understand why he wanted a baby, even if *he* didn't comprehend *her* reasons.

But she couldn't give up her baby any more than he could.

She squared her shoulders and picked up the phone. She was going to have her baby.

She dialed the number written on the pad. After a

conversation with the fertility clinic in Denver, she felt a little better.

Life was strange. Lucas Boyd had had all the things she wanted. Now, he was no better off than she was. Indeed, he was worse off, because he couldn't have his child.

She emerged from her office and Abby immediately searched her face.

"I'm fine." She even added a smile.

"If Luke insulted you, or hurt you, you tell me, girl. I love that boy, but I won't tolerate him not treating you with respect."

Susannah chuckled. Abby's normally serene eyes were agitated and her lips were pressed together. It would be fun to see her take on Lucas Boyd. But Susannah couldn't lie. "He didn't hurt me, Abby. It was a misunderstanding, and he came to offer his apology."

"An apology that made you cry?" she asked skeptically.

"I—I felt sorry for him. It's so sad that his wife and child died."

Abby didn't look convinced but she didn't ask any more questions. Unfortunately she turned to the one subject Susannah wanted to avoid more than Lucas Boyd. "What are you going to do about this baby thing?"

"Exactly what I planned to do. I called the clinic in Denver and I have an appointment next Friday for my initial examination."

"You're going to close the library?"

Friday was their second busiest day, but Susannah

didn't want to postpone the appointment. "No, I'm hoping to talk you and another volunteer into covering for me. Would you, please, Abby? I don't want to wait."

Since today was Friday, she already had to wait seven days. Seven long days. What if she discovered she couldn't have children? Then she'd be just as bad off as Lucas Boyd.

Stop thinking about that man.

Easier said than done. He would be many a woman's dream of Prince Charming. Prince Charming with an attitude. He was one of those men who thought women should be barefoot and pregnant.

"I still think you could find a man around here interested in settling down if you'd just make a little more effort," Abby insisted. "Are you coming tomorrow night?"

"I don't think so, Abby. I don't know how to dance, and I won't have time to bake something."

"I'll bake double. You promised me you'd come to the next social." Abby had the determined look of a dog after a bone. "It seems a fair trade for keeping the library open for you next Friday."

"That's blackmail, Abigail!"

"Yep. Well? Is it working?"

She had promised. And she did need Abby's help. "Yes, I suppose so. But I'll do my own baking."

"Just as well. The only thing I ever bake is a pecan cake. If you brought one, everyone would know I made it. Then folks would think you couldn't cook. Can't catch a man that way!"

"Abby! I'm coming to be sociable, not to find a

man. I've already made my decision." She stared at her friend, trying to make her position clear.

Abby turned limpid hazel eyes on her and said with a sugary voice, "Why, of course, Susannah. Just what I had in mind."

Patting her gray hair, Abby slid off the stool behind the counter. "I'd better hurry home if I'm going to get my cake made tonight. Don't you work late, either."

"No, I won't." She had too much to do, what with baking a dessert for the church social and preparing herself, mentally at least, for next Friday's date.

"Oh," Abby said as she paused by the front door, "wear your prettiest dress, too."

"Abby!" Susannah warned, but her friend was out the door with a wave.

Abby never gave up. At least she believed someday a man might be attracted to her friend. That was more than Susannah believed. But Abby's faith was comforting.

Lucas surveyed himself in the mirror. Since he'd made his decision, he'd spent more time looking at himself than he had in years.

Was he dressed all right? His jeans were clean, his shirt pressed. The sports coat, kind of tweedy, still fit, though it wasn't new. Beth had picked it out for him.

He ran his fingers over its lapel, his mind turning once more to his wife. They'd only been married a little over a year. She had been ten years younger than he, just a kid, when he'd fallen for her. Her folks lived on a farm close to town. She'd loved the ranch, the big house, lots of money to spend.

That was what he missed most. The way she'd enjoyed life. His dad had been sick the past two years, and Lucas had forgotten how to smile. When Beth came into his life, suddenly sunshine was everywhere.

For the past three years, it felt as if he'd been living in a cave.

Well, tonight was his coming out party. Doc had persuaded him to try his plan. Lucas still wasn't convinced he could go through with it. But it did make sense.

He turned away from the mirror. His looks didn't matter. And neither did memories. He needed to be practical.

When he entered the kitchen, Frankie was sweeping the room. "Did you fix a dish for me to take, Frankie?"

"Yeah, boss, but you know you don't have to take anything. It's the womenfolk that bring the food." While he spoke, Frankie's gaze was running up and down him.

"Is something wrong with the way I look?"

"Naw. You look real purty!" Frankie assured him with a chuckle.

"Watch it, you mangy coyote, or I'll tell Mrs. Appleworth that you're longing for her company."

Frankie shivered with fear. Mrs. Appleworth, already having married five times, was known for her interest in cowboys. "That lady would have me hightailin' it out of the county, boss. And then who would cook and clean for an ornery cuss like you?''

"Okay, point taken. I'll see you tomorrow," he assured his cook and picked up the large bowl filled with potato salad. At least he'd gotten by Frankie without him commenting on his boss attending the party. Lucas hoped his entry would be noticed as little.

He'd timed his arrival for after the party had gotten into full swing, figuring he'd slip into the room while no one was looking.

Instead the music had just ended and suddenly it seemed everyone was staring at him. Then there was a concerted rush forward to greet him. Damn! You'd think he'd been in hibernation for a century.

"Luke! Good to see you! Didn't know you were venturing out," one neighbor said. Another commented on the last time he'd seen him, then hastily broke off his words because it had been the occasion of Beth and the baby's funeral.

Someone else hurriedly asked about a problem on the ranch. One of the ladies took his bowl from him with a gracious smile, and then Doc took him by the arm and drew him into the big room.

He wanted to run the other way. Small talk was beyond him tonight. He had too much on his mind. Doc seemed to realize how he felt.

"You did fine, boy. First step's the hardest. She's already here, and lookin' real nice. See her? On the other side of the room with Abby.''

He saw her. Susannah Langston did look nice. She wore a blouse that fitted her curves, surprising him, and a full skirt. And he'd been wrong. She didn't have fat ankles.

The music started up again.

"Go ask her to dance," Doc urged in a whisper.

"I just got here, Doc."

"Never mind. It's too late now."

His head whipped around and he stared at the cowboy who was leading the librarian onto the floor. Max Daingerfield. He was a wiry cowboy from north of town who considered himself to be the life of the party. Sometimes he was a little too lively for the other guests.

Lucas clenched his teeth as he watched the man's arm snake around Susannah's waist and haul her up against him. Then he relaxed with a smile as the lady removed the cowboy's hand from her hip, took a step away from him and made a brief remark.

At least Susannah was no more compliant with Max than she'd been with him.

"Hey, Lucas, heard you bought a new stallion," one of his neighbors said, drawing his attention from the couple on the floor. Soon he found himself drawn into ranch talk, almost forgetting his reason for attending the party.

"Aren't you gonna dance with her?" Doc finally whispered, as he dug his finger into Lucas's side.

"What'd you say, Doc?" Joe Springer asked, standing beside Lucas.

"I was just suggesting Luke have a dance. If he can still remember how."

Joe laughed. "I reckon it's like a few other

things,'' he said with a wink. ''Once you learn, you don't forget.''

Lucas didn't want to follow Doc's suggestion. But he'd promised himself he'd give it the old college try. He surveyed the room and found Susannah leaving the dance floor with another partner. Had she danced every dance? Why was she looking for a donor if she could have her pick of men?

That thought didn't make him too happy. He stomped across the room and hauled up in front of her. ''Evening, Susannah. Want to dance?''

''Thank you, but I imagine I've mangled enough toes this evening.'' She smiled but it wasn't with the same warmth as he'd seen earlier.

He couldn't believe she was turning him down.

The music started and he reached down for her hand. ''I think my toes can handle the torture.''

''Mr. Boyd, I don't want to dance with you!'' she whispered as he pulled her to her feet.

''I kind of gathered that when you said no. But it'll be a little too embarrassing to face everyone now. So I reckon you'll dance whether you like it or not.''

She looked over his shoulder and then back to his face. ''Everyone's watching us.''

''I know. Unfortunately for you, this is the first time I've danced with anyone since—in a long time. That's why I couldn't just walk away. Sorry.''

His voice was gruff, but she didn't seem to take offense. She tentatively put her hand on his shoulder as he began to move to the waltz.

"I'm not going to bite you," he growled and pulled her a little closer.

"I didn't think you would, but I don't like to dance so close," she informed him in a schoolteacher voice.

He grinned. "I know. I watched you straighten Max out."

She leaned back and caught his grin. "Is he a friend of yours?"

"Nope."

"Ah."

Neither spoke for several minutes. Lucas noticed how small her waist was, how neatly she fit into his arms, the top of her head right next to his cheekbone. He even noticed how good she smelled. Like springtime in the mountains.

Beth had always worn a heavy scent, too sophisticated for—he'd promised himself he wouldn't think about Beth. Not tonight.

"You haven't managed to stumble over my toes yet," he muttered, pulling her just that little bit closer, so that her breasts brushed against his chest when they turned. His groin tightened and he was suddenly very conscious that he was a man...and that Susannah was a desirable woman.

"I guess you're lucky," she said, her voice breathless, as if she'd been running a race.

"You tired?" he asked, frowning down at her. If she was in such bad shape, how would she handle having a baby? But she didn't look weak.

She took a step back from him. "No, I'm fine. And the dance is almost over."

"Counting the minutes, huh? Maybe I should tell you *some* women around here are eager to dance with me." He hadn't meant to sound so cocky, but she'd damaged his ego with her reluctance.

She lifted her chin and met his gaze. "How would you know, Mr. Boyd? According to you this is your first dance in three years. Maybe local taste has changed."

He gave a cynical chuckle. "Money never goes out of style, Susannah, so I reckon I'm safe."

"Is that why Beth married you?" she retorted and then gasped. "I'm sorry. I shouldn't have—I let my temper—I'm sorry."

He'd stiffened in rage, but her immediate apology had made it impossible to vent his anger. So he clenched his jaw and continued to dance.

"Mr. Boyd, that was horribly rude of me. I'm sure your wife loved you very much. I—"

"You don't know anything about Beth, Miss Langston, so keep your comments to yourself."

And she did.

They circled the room, in each other's arms, not speaking. Lucas regretted his rough words, but he was still angry. When the music ended with a flourish, the leader, Red Jones, stepped to the mike. "Grab your partner, fellas, and head for the tables. There's good food awaitin'!"

Susannah acted as if she hadn't heard the man's words. She started away from Lucas as if walking away from a car she'd parked. He grabbed her arm.

"Didn't you hear the man?"

She looked as pale as when she'd first stood in his

living room, but her gaze was harder. "I assumed that was a suggestion, not an order."

"Well, we're going to follow it, whatever it was. You'll eat with me," he said sternly, urging her on.

She came to a complete halt. "Mr. Boyd, you have a distressing habit of issuing orders and expecting me to comply with them. In case you haven't noticed, servitude has gone out of fashion. So has manhandling a woman in public. Now, excuse me." She jerked her arm from his hand and gracefully crossed the room to Abby's side behind one of the tables.

In the rush for food, Lucas didn't think anyone noticed his partner abandoning him in the middle of the floor, but he was still angry. He casually strolled over to several of the men talking and joined the conversation. But he watched Susannah Langston out of the corner of his eye.

Which is probably why he didn't notice Abby approaching.

"Lucas Boyd, I want a word with you!"

"Uh-oh, Luke," Joe said, "you'd better watch out. I think Abby's on the warpath."

"You'd better be scared, all of you, since I remember changing your diapers!" she said, glaring at the four men. Then she grabbed Lucas's arm and tugged him in the direction of the open door.

He was reminded of Susannah's words when he'd tried the same thing with her, but he didn't think Abby would pay any attention. "What's wrong, Abby?"

"Wait till we're outside. I don't want anyone overhearing us."

They stepped out into the clear, crisp October night. After they'd gone past several parked cars, she turned to face him. "What did you say to hurt Susannah?"

"Me? She's the one who said something! Hell, she said Beth married me for my money, Abby!" He hadn't intended to repeat the idiotic words, but he hadn't realized how deeply they'd cut him.

"Susannah wouldn't do that, Luke. Why, she's the gentlest, kindest—"

"I'm tired of everybody saying that. She's not gentle or kind with me." He crossed his arms over his chest. Saint Susannah didn't exist as far as he was concerned.

"You must've said something mean for her to try to hurt you. What did you say first?"

"I asked her to dance. Is that a crime?"

"No. But you must be wanting something she can't—"

"Abby, this is ridiculous. I didn't do anything."

"Then what did you want from her? When you came to the library yesterday, you did something to upset her then, too. She was almost in tears."

Lucas's nerves were stretched tight, what with his appearance among his neighbors this evening, and his plans for the future. Suddenly he couldn't stand Abby's prying any longer. With a roar, he said, "I want her to have my baby, Abby. That's what I want!"

Unfortunately, several other couples had also come outside for the cool air. They all froze as his words rang in the air.

Then there was a concerted rush back inside, each hoping to be the first to pass on the delicious gossip they'd just overheard.

Chapter Four

Susannah stood near one of the serving tables, chatting with several ladies who frequented the library. Even so, she kept her eye on the door, watching for Abby and Lucas's return.

It didn't take long for her to realize something had happened outside that was causing a lot of excitement. Three or four people rushed in and immediately began whispering.

When everyone who heard the gossip turned to stare at Susannah, she knew she was in trouble.

"What's goin' on?" Mrs. Wilson wondered, staring across the room.

"I have no idea," Susannah said, then fell silent. Abby and Lucas Boyd entered the room.

"There's Abby. I bet she'll know. Yoo-hoo, Abby!" Mrs. Wilson called across the room.

Wishing the floor would open and swallow her whole, Susannah stepped away from her acquaintance. Suddenly she didn't want to know what was causing all the ruckus. Because it involved her...and Lucas Boyd.

Whether it was in response to Mrs. Wilson's call, or something else, Abby started across the room, determination in her every step.

Followed by Lucas Boyd.

And the gazes of everyone in the room.

Susannah stood frozen, unable to escape or think. She never liked to be in the spotlight, but when Lucas Boyd was involved, she became absolutely paralyzed.

Abby reached her and clutched her hand, as if to comfort her. "Lucas didn't mean no harm, Susannah."

Considering her friend's words, Susannah looked at the handsome cowboy, surprised to discover his lean cheeks filled with color. "About what?"

Vaguely, out of the corner of her eye, she noticed Mrs. Wilson whispering with another woman. Before either Abby or Lucas was able or willing to answer her question, Mrs. Wilson turned to her.

"Oh, I'm thrilled. I mean, I had no idea! Why didn't you let on, Susannah? Why, you've caught the most eligible man in the county!"

Dread filled Susannah. She'd been right to be afraid. Taking a deep breath, she said, as calmly as possible, "I haven't caught anything, Mrs. Wilson. There must be some mistake."

With an arch laugh that grated on Susannah's nerves, Mrs. Wilson said, "Well, I hope you've caught him if you're going to have his baby!"

Susannah let her eyelids sink, shutting out everything. When she opened them again, she had no clue what she should do or say. Especially when she still didn't know exactly what had been said. But now wasn't the time to be asking. A quick glance at Abby and Lucas Boyd showed them frozen. "There's been some mistake, Mrs. Wilson."

She couldn't go on. How could she explain about *her* baby, without everyone thinking it was *his* baby? They'd never believe the scientific arrangements she'd made. It would be so much more fun for them to speculate on her sleeping with Lucas Boyd. The man had ruined everything!

The plate she was holding, filled with various samplings of the delicious food, held no interest for her now. With a rigid smile, she set it on the edge of the table. "Excuse me, please," she murmured and turned to head for the rest room.

"Susannah—" Abby called.

Susannah didn't turn around, but she heard footsteps behind her and hoped they were Abby's, not the cowboy's. She thought if he touched her now, she'd scream.

She slipped into the small rest room and entered a stall, closing the door, hoping Abby would allow her some privacy. No such luck.

"Susannah, he didn't mean to embarrass you. It's partly my fault."

"Abby, could this discussion wait—"

"No. I'm trying to tell you it was an accident. He didn't mean to announce that you were going to have his baby."

"He did what?" she gasped, unable to remain silent.

The stall next to her opened. "Who did?" a quavery voice asked. "Is someone pregnant?"

"Now, Gertie, I didn't know you were here. This is a private conversation," Abby hastily said.

Susannah leaned her head against the door, trying to hold back a moan. Gertie Lumpkin was probably the only one who hadn't heard what happened. Until now.

"Don't seem too private if he announced it. I just want to know who he is."

"Abby, don't—"

The door squeaked as two women entered. "Oh, here you are, Abby. Where's Susannah?" one asked with a giggle.

Abby remained silent but Gertie didn't. "She's in there, I think."

"Susannah? Come on out. We want to congratulate you!"

"You're supposed to offer best wishes to the bride and congratulate the groom," Gertie instructed.

The second voice, which Susannah couldn't identify, either, protested, "Honey, if she's getting Lucas Boyd to the altar again, she deserves congratulations!"

"Is she in here?" someone called as the door squeaked again. There was a rush of footsteps, telling Susannah more than one lady had swelled the ranks.

Lifting her chin, Susannah opened the stall door. "Sorry, I didn't mean to keep everyone waiting.

Whoever's next," she said and waved to the stall behind her.

"Is it true?" a young woman asked, a pout on her lips. "Have you lassoed Lucas Boyd?"

"I don't think so. I don't even have a rope," Susannah said with a smile. A weak smile, but still a smile. "I only met the man a couple of weeks ago. If he's looking for a wife, you know he's going to choose one a lot prettier than me."

With a nod, she began to push through the women, ignoring their startled looks. Abby was right behind her.

As soon as they were in the hall, Susannah whispered, "Is there a back way out of here?"

"No. And you got no reason to hide, Susannah. But tell me, is what he said true? Are you going to have his baby?" Abby was watching her anxiously.

She covered her face with her hands and then looked at Abby. "Are you sure that's what he said?"

"Well, he said he *wanted* you to."

"No. I'm not going to have his baby. Dr. Grable...Lucas thought...never mind. The answer is no."

When she walked back into the large room, everyone stood clustered in groups, talking. Until they saw her.

Silence filled the room.

She felt the heat building in her cheeks, but she pretended all was well. Pausing by one of the committee members who organized the social, she offered her thanks for a lovely evening, shaking the woman's hand.

"Are you leaving?"

"I have to be up early for Sunday School, so I think I'll call it a night," Susannah said.

"Lucas already left."

Susannah licked her dry lips. "Lucas? Oh, you mean Lucas Boyd. Did he? Maybe he's teaching a Sunday School class, too."

There was a ripple of laughter at her words, indicating more than a few were listening. She maintained her friendly smile with some effort and started toward the door, bravely meeting the stares and nodding.

Abby plucked at her sleeve when she reached the door, almost free to hide in the darkness of the night. "Don't be mad at Lucas, Susannah. It was partly my fault. I wish you'd stay a while longer."

Susannah looked down at her dearest friend. "I don't think so, Abby. But thank you for inviting me." She pulled free from Abby's grasp and hurried down the stairs. Her car was parked along the side of the building, out of sight. She breathed a sigh of relief as she turned the corner.

Until she caught sight of her car.

And her nemesis leaning against it.

Lucas feared she was going to run in the opposite direction when she saw him. He wanted to talk to her, but he wouldn't be able to chase her here. Everyone would be watching them.

But instead of running, the woman started walking toward her car again, her gaze on the ground.

"Susannah," he began, keeping his voice quiet.

"Please move," she ordered.

He'd blocked her door on purpose. He wasn't about to abandon his position of strength before he'd had his say. "I want to apologize. I lost my temper."

"Did someone refuse to follow your orders?"

He couldn't believe her cool challenge. He'd been prepared to grovel because he figured he'd upset her, maybe made her cry. A gentleman didn't cause a lady grief. But her cool voice, challenging him, didn't inspire him to wallow in remorse.

"No," he responded through gritted teeth. "But your behavior certainly didn't help."

Her chin rose slightly. "My behavior was exemplary."

"Oh, yeah? You walked off and left me standing like a fool on the dance floor!" His fists went to his hips and he glared down at her. Not too far down.

"The last I heard, a woman has a choice about her dinner companion."

"There was no call to embarrass me."

"Is that why you said what you did? To pay me back? You certainly accomplished your goal, Mr. Boyd."

He felt a few inches shorter at her words. "No! No, I wasn't trying to embarrass you, Susannah. I promise. Abby was pressing me about—about upsetting you. Did I upset you?"

"I don't find it charming to be the object of gossip, Mr. Boyd."

"Before that. While we were dancing. Abby said she thought I'd upset you." He watched her face carefully, seeing changing emotions reflected in her eyes. Her full bottom lip trembled slightly. He'd never have noticed if he hadn't been watching so closely.

She looked over his shoulder. "I was embarrassed that I had behaved so rudely. I never meant to insult your wife or imply that your marriage was—was less than a love match. Abby interpreted my embarrassment as something else." She brought her brown-eyed gaze back to him. "I suppose I owe you an apology also."

She amazed him. He'd never expected her to apologize. In his experience, women accepted apologies well. But they weren't in the habit of owning up to any guilt for an argument. Some of the tension flowed out of him.

"Thanks, Susannah. I guess neither of us showed our best social skills this evening. I don't know about your excuse, but I'm a little out of practice." He tried a smile, curious to see if she'd give him one back.

She didn't.

"Now that we've finished our discussion, could you move so I can get in my car?" She stared at his boots.

"Well, I would," he drawled, watching her, "but I don't think we're finished."

His words drew a flash of her brown eyes filled with questions and not a little alarm. "What do you mean? Of course we're finished."

"Nope. We have to decide what we're going to do about my little mistake." He crossed his arms over his chest, as if he intended to remain in place for the next century.

Any softness, or sympathetic feelings, he'd thought he'd seen in her apology disappeared. "We're going to do nothing, Mr. Boyd. Absolutely nothing."

"Don't you think you could call me Lucas? After all, since everyone thinks we're already sleeping together, being formal seems a mite silly."

She gasped. "All the more reason to remain formal. And to avoid each other. All we have to do is go back to our normal routines. You avoid the library. I'll avoid your ranch. Problem solved."

Rubbing the back of his neck, Lucas asked her another question. "You still going to have a baby?"

"Of course I am!"

"You know people are going to say it's mine." This time he held her gaze, waiting for her reaction.

"If—if we continue to deny it and aren't seen together, I'm sure that rumor will disappear... eventually."

Again there was that slight tremble of her bottom lip. He wanted to reach out and stroke its softness. Reassure her. "Maybe."

"I need to go home. I'm cold."

Now he had no choice but to move aside. Any other woman, he might offer to warm her up. But Susannah had suffered enough tonight at his hands. He wouldn't make things worse. But he was surprised at the disappointment that filled him.

He must've been too long without a woman.

But thoughts of Beth had made the idea of seeking physical relief impossible. He couldn't imagine holding another woman in his arms.

Turning, he opened the car door and held it for her. She slid past him, leaving as much room as possible between them, murmuring a thank-you.

Before he closed the door, he said, "I have another idea, Susannah. I'll explain it to you tomorrow."

"No! We're supposed to avoid each other."

The panic on her face gave him pause. Maybe she wasn't as calm about all this as she pretended to be. He grinned. "Don't worry, sugar. I'll be discreet."

Her only response was to slam the door and gun the engine, her tires spraying gravel, and shoot out of the parking lot.

Luckily Lucas was fast on his feet or he might have had tire tracks on his boots.

Discreet? The man didn't know the meaning of the word. It was because of his indiscretion that she had a headache now.

That and his sex appeal. She'd almost lost her footing when her breasts had pressed against his chest while they were dancing. She'd never experienced such a flood of wanting in her life.

Susannah clenched her teeth as she drove to the small house she leased from Abby. When she got out of the car, she unlocked her door and entered, throwing her purse and keys on the sofa. Then she paced the room, suddenly wishing it were larger.

What was she going to do now?

If she went ahead with her plan, everyone would assume she was having Lucas's baby, as he'd said. If she didn't, she'd miss out on the one thing she longed for.

As she strode around the room, she discarded several different ideas. Then the most logical response filled her head.

Of course! The best answer would be to find someone else for Lucas Boyd. Every woman there tonight had shown an interest in the wealthy, handsome rancher. All she, Susannah, had to do was turn one, or even two, loose on him. Soon she'd be completely forgotten.

Relieved that she'd come up with a solution, she sat down at the small desk her grandmother had once owned and took out the elegant cream stationery she seldom used. After writing a careful note, she reread it.

Yes, this should do the trick.

But she'd have to work fast before he turned up at the library again.

Sunday afternoon, Lucas was putting in time at his desk, trying to catch up on the mountain of paperwork involved in running a ranch.

Someone knocked on his door. "Come in," he shouted, his gaze glued to his paperwork.

Frankie walked in.

"Yeah?" His housekeeper seldom interrupted Lucas when he was doing the books.

"Sam Jenkins stopped by. Wanted me to give you this letter. Said someone asked him to drop it off after church."

He took the envelope, studying it curiously. "Thanks," he muttered and laid it aside.

He didn't remember the envelope for several

hours. Then, as he finished paying the bills for the month, he noticed the envelope he'd put to one side.

Frowning, he picked it up. His name was on it, but nothing else, no address. Sam Jenkins? His neighbor didn't seem the type to use such nice stationery, but maybe his wife was having a party. Lucas supposed his emergence into local society last night might draw a few invitations.

Inside, he didn't find an invitation. His gaze flew to the bottom where Susannah Langston's signature grabbed his attention.

Dear Lucas,
I think I've come up with a plan to solve our little difficulty. Could you meet me for lunch tomorrow at The Red Slipper? At noon, please.

She didn't know much about ranchers if she thought they went to town for lunch in the middle of the day. But he'd make an exception for her. Later, he'd explain that you didn't interrupt a man's day for little things.

A smile settled on his lips as he thought about the meaning of her note. There was only one solution, as far as he was concerned, but he'd be glad to listen to Susannah's version. After all, he was flexible.

Now he could make real plans for his son. And he could forget Doc's scheme. He hadn't been comfortable with the idea of marrying anyone, much less Susannah Langston. True, she was more attractive than he'd first thought. A lot more attractive. But she always argued with him.

She wouldn't be a good wife because of that, but she'd make a damn fine baby for him. A tall, strong son, determined and courageous. Yeah, she'd be a great mother.

He could hardly wait until tomorrow.

Lucas came in from the pastures at about ten-thirty the next morning. He felt pretty silly showering in the middle of the day, but you couldn't have lunch with a lady when you smelled of horse.

All morning he'd thought about Susannah's note. Celebrated it. And ignored the small worrisome nudge that the sweetness and light routine it projected wasn't like her. That had occurred to him just before he went to sleep last night, and it had taken him a while to put it aside.

She was probably happy because she was going to have a baby. That's all it was. Her dream was going to be achieved, just like his. She'd probably decided to accept his offer of taking care of his son after he was born.

His son.

Those two words danced in his heart, giving him such pleasure. He almost forgot the woman who would make his dream happen. Almost.

She'd been pretty angry Saturday night. But her note showed that she'd gotten over her anger. He liked that, someone who didn't hold a grudge.

He dressed with extra care. At this rate, he'd have to go shopping for some new shirts and jeans. His social life seemed to be on the upswing.

With a grin, he grabbed a jacket and headed down

the stairs. When he passed Frankie, he said, "I'm lunching at The Red Slipper with a lady, Frankie. I'll be back later."

The man was too stunned to say anything, and Lucas left with a smile on his face. Wait until he could tell Frankie about his son!

It was a short drive into Caliente, and he quickly parked the truck among the many others around The Red Slipper. There weren't too many dining choices in town. The Red Slipper was the best of the lot.

The hostess met him at the door with a grin. "Howdy, Luke. I heard you were coming today."

"Oh, really? Word travels fast." He didn't mind. Soon he'd be able to tell everyone his secret.

"Just follow me."

He took off his hat and weaved between the tables, searching for Susannah. When he couldn't see her anywhere, he assumed the hostess was taking him to an empty table to wait for her. Instead the woman stopped unexpectedly and Lucas almost ran over her.

"Here you go, Lucas. Enjoy your meal, ladies."

Lucas stood there as if he'd been poleaxed. Staring up at him with eager faces were three blondes, all waiting for him to sit down beside them.

Chapter Five

Susannah was feeling quite satisfied with herself.

Not only had she figured out how to end the speculation about any baby she might have, but she'd also managed to pull it off quickly.

It hadn't been easy to locate three petite blondes in Caliente. Since Lucas Boyd had fallen for that type the first time, it made sense to Susannah that he'd most likely follow the same pattern now. With Abby's help, she'd located the three most attractive ladies.

But that had only been the beginning. Then she had to convince them to share their moment with Lucas Boyd with each other. None of them liked the idea.

In the end, however, they'd all agreed, because they wanted first crack at a wealthy widower who'd finally come out of seclusion.

"Did you hear?" Gertie asked as she tottered up

to the front desk in the library, two books clutched against her sagging bustline.

"I beg your pardon, Gertie? Did I hear what?" Susannah asked, somewhat distracted by her thoughts.

"Lucas Boyd. He's eatin' at The Red Slipper with three women," the little lady said, as if she were revealing a secret liaison between China and Russia.

"Really?" Susannah said nonchalantly. "Well, I guess my heart is broken."

Gertie peered at her. "You don't look too upset."

"I'm a great actress. I hide my feelings well." Susannah added a grin so the old lady would realize she was teasing.

"Humph. Lucas is a good catch."

"Yes, I believe he is, but I'm not fishing." She held out her hand for the lady's choices and proceeded to stamp them and then hand them back. Gertie was known for her gossiping. If she believed there was nothing between Lucas and Susannah, the entire town would know it at once.

"Well, you ought to be trying to catch someone. Ladies need husbands," Gertie muttered, ignoring the fact that she'd been widowed twenty-two years ago and managed just fine.

"Maybe you should go after Lucas, Gertie. He'd make you a fine—"

Susannah's teasing smile was wiped from her face as the library's front door, an antique in oak with flawlessly etched glass, was slammed against the outside wall.

Even more disturbing was the angry man standing

just inside. His cowboy hat was jammed low on his forehead, shadowing his face, but Susannah had no difficulty identifying him. Or the mood he was in.

"Oh, my," Gertie whispered, staring.

Susannah fought the urge to run. She'd known that Lucas Boyd might initially have been unhappy with her scheme, but she'd counted on the ladies to charm him.

She'd miscalculated.

He strode up to the checkout counter and gestured behind her. "In your office!" Then, without waiting to see if she complied, he marched around the counter and through her office door.

Gertie's eyes were wide as she swung her gaze back to Susannah. "What's going on?"

"Um, I think Mr. Boyd has an overdue book," she offered, though she knew her answer was nonsensical. She gestured to one of her volunteers to come take her place at the front desk. "Excuse me, Gertie. I hope you enjoy your books."

The little lady didn't take the hint, not budging one inch from her front row stance. "You going to go talk to him?"

"Well, yes, as librarian, I—"

"Susannah, get in here!" Lucas roared.

That did it! She didn't often lose her temper, but if that man thought... Without finishing her response to Gertie, she slid from the stool and crossed the short distance to her small office.

After carefully closing the door, she whirled around. "How dare you?"

"How dare *you!*" he returned.

He was standing with his fists cocked on his hips, his lips pressed tightly together, a frown on his brow. And his hat was still on. Susannah felt her heart racing wildly and wondered if it was his anger...or his potent virility that caused all her senses to quicken.

"All I did was arrange a luncheon so you could meet some nice ladies," she said, primly, and perhaps not quite truthfully.

"All you did was feed me to three female barracudas in front of the entire town!"

"That's not a gentlemanly remark," she protested. As he opened his mouth to respond, she hurriedly added, "They are all beautiful blondes. I thought you liked blondes."

"Two of them aren't blondes. Lisa's been bleaching her hair since she was fourteen, and it looks like straw by now. Belinda bleached hers when she got her first divorce."

Susannah blinked in surprise. "I didn't know you were such a purist, or knew the ladies that well."

"Hell, of course I know them. They've lived here all their lives. Now, you tell me what kind of game you're playing." He took a step closer to her.

Backing until she was plastered against the door she'd just closed, Susannah drew a deep breath. She wanted to avoid his touch at all costs—it would never do for him to realize the bone-melting effect he had on her. "I thought the debacle Saturday night would be best handled by your showing some interest in—in other women."

"And you didn't think it necessary to inform me

of your little plan?'' he asked, his soft tones more threatening than his earlier yelling.

Susannah wished she had more room to maneuver. ''N-no. I didn't think you'd cooperate.''

''Damn right I wouldn't cooperate. Those women thought I was going to marry one of them,'' he growled.

''Wouldn't that solve your problem?''

His hands shot forward to trap her against the door. ''No, ma'am, that wouldn't solve my problem.''

''I don't see why not. You would have your son—''

''And a wife I don't want.''

Susannah nervously chewed on her bottom lip as she tried to come up with another answer, but her mind was blank. It was hard to think with two hundred pounds of sexy, angry cowboy hovering over you.

''Damn! Stop that!''

Her eyes widened and she stared at him, at a loss. ''What? Stop what?''

''Chewing on your lip,'' he informed her as he turned his back on her and took several steps away. He tried to relax the muscles that had tightened in his gut when he saw her nibbling on those soft lips. A softness he had wanted to test with his own lips.

She didn't really understand his concern with her lip, but if it convinced him to give her some breathing space, she wasn't going to complain. ''I'm sorry if—if you had a difficult time at lunch. I did pay for it.''

He whirled around to glare at her. "Yeah. That really made me feel good. A woman paying my way!"

"You really are a macho man, aren't you?" She didn't think he'd be under any illusions that she was paying him a compliment. "Of course I paid. I extended the invitation."

"A bogus invitation. I thought you were going to agree to—you know."

His gaze shifted away from her, but not before Susannah caught a glimpse of the sadness and hurt inside him. She hadn't intended to be mean. Without thinking, she reached out to pat his shoulder. He jerked back as if he'd been stung.

"I wanted to say I'm sorry," she explained stiffly. Okay, he didn't want her to touch him. She could certainly understand that reaction, but she'd only meant to be gracious. "I didn't intend to hurt you."

"Yeah, right."

"Really. I thought you might like one of those ladies. I tried to find some who looked like Beth because—"

"Don't you mention her name with those three! You know nothing about Beth. She was—was perfect! I'll never love anyone like I loved Beth. And don't you forget it!"

Susannah jumped aside as Lucas rushed out of her office. He didn't pause to greet any neighbors in his flight from the library. Even Gertie.

Who was still standing next to the front desk, watching Lucas's exit.

"Gertie. I didn't know you were still here," Su-

sannah said, forcing her voice to sound normal.
"Were there some other books you were interested
in?"

With a sly grin, the little old lady shook her head.
"Nope. I was just passing the time of day with
Louisa, here," she said, gesturing to the volunteer
who'd replaced Susannah.

"Ah. Louisa, could you hold down the fort a while
longer. I have some paperwork I need to take care
of."

"Of course, Susannah. I'm here for another hour.
Take your time." Then the woman exchanged a look
with Gertie.

Unable to deal with anything else at the moment,
Susannah murmured her thanks and retreated into her
office, closing the door behind her. She felt like an
animal who needed privacy to lick her wounds. The
cowboy's pain echoed in her heart. And she didn't
know what she was going to do now.

Time to reevaluate her plans. Lucas Boyd wasn't
cooperating.

Word spread like wildfire through the small community. First, Lucas's unexpected luncheon with
three blondes. Then his visit to the library. When the
men of Caliente came to their dinner tables that evening, their wives were primed to entertain them with
the excitement of the day.

Lucas's hopes that other, more exciting develop-
ments would occur to dismiss his antics were dashed
when his phone rang after dinner.

"Boy, what are you up to?"

He didn't need the caller to identify himself. "Hi, Doc. What do you mean?"

"You interested in one of those women? They're all wrong for you."

Lucas sighed. "I'm not playing the dating game, Doc. Calm down."

"Then why—"

"It's all your fault," Lucas assured him, a grim smile on his lips.

"What are you talking about? I didn't have anything to do with it."

"No, not directly. But Susannah Langston, that sweet, angelic lady, did. She trapped me without me having any idea what was coming."

Heavy silence followed his words. Finally Doc said, "What do you mean?"

"She wrote me a note, saying she had a solution to our difficulties, asked me to meet her for lunch at The Red Slipper today. When I arrived, those three were waiting for me. And the lovely Miss Langston even paid the bill."

"Oh, my. I guess that explains the second part of the gossip. You went to the library to tear a strip off her hide, didn't you?"

Lucas sighed again. He regretted his impulsive behavior, but after an hour fending off the blatant seduction of three women at once, he'd been ready to vent. "Yeah, I'm afraid so."

More silence.

Finally Doc asked, "So, are you abandoning our plan?"

Groaning, Lucas shook his head, then realized Doc couldn't see his response. "I don't know, Doc."

"Hell, you knew it wasn't going to be easy."

"Easy? True, but I didn't expect to have to survive anything like that lunch today. Those women were in a feeding frenzy. I was a big fat lunch ticket, and they were willing to do anything to seal the bargain. I've never been so embarrassed in my life."

"What did they do?"

"Other than run their hands all over me under the table? Of course, Doreen, since she was seated across from me, had to use her toes, but that didn't slow her down. Let's see, they offered some comfort in the dark, without the others, in various ways."

He closed his eyes as he thought of their blatant overtures. "They all expressed sympathy that I'd been without a woman for such a long time." As if sex were nothing more than a creature comfort.

"And you weren't tempted?"

That question stopped Lucas cold. Because he had been tempted and he'd tried to forget that part.

It wasn't the blondes who had tempted him, however. To his amazement, Susannah with fear in her eyes and chewing on her soft lip, had aroused desire. His gut had clenched and he'd fought the temptation to reach out and stroke her face.

"Those ladies didn't tempt me," he finally said.

"So what are you going to do?"

Lucas had given that question a lot of thought. He still wanted a son. His disappointment had been immense when he'd realized the local librarian had tricked him. But he couldn't abandon his plan. Or rather Doc's plan.

"I've got to do some more thinking, Doc. I don't know if I can carry your idea off."

"All you have to do is be honest, boy. Explain what you're offering, pure and simple. That shouldn't be so hard."

Lucas's gut tightened again, but it wasn't from fear of being honest. No, it was from fear of losing control, of being too attracted to the woman, of wanting too much. He had to stay focused on his child and forget Susannah.

The next day, Susannah knew her plan had backfired on her by all the curious stares of the patrons of the Caliente Library. Some of the visitors had never darkened the library's door before. They all wanted to see the woman who had spit in the wind, trod on Superman's cape and messed with Bad Leroy Brown. Or, in this case, Lucas Boyd.

In other words, instead of making people forget she was connected to Lucas, she'd only reminded them. Or rather, Lucas's reaction to her plan had done so.

With a quickly subdued sigh, she smiled at the old rancher who requested books on Colorado history and led him to the proper section. She supposed she should be grateful. The increase in usage of books would impress the city council.

"My, we're busy today," Abby said as she rounded the counter. "Haven't seen this many people here since we opened the place."

"Yes. The people of Caliente are certainly eager to learn today," Susannah said, unable to keep a touch of sarcasm from her voice.

Abby smirked. She'd warned Susannah that her plan might go awry. So far she hadn't said the fatal words, "I told you so," but Susannah was expecting them at any moment.

"They're just showing a little interest in their community," Abby assured her with a wider grin.

Susannah remembered Lucas's words of disbelief and used them herself. "Yeah, right."

Unfortunately for her, she hadn't been able to forget a single word the man had said. She supposed it was only fair that she use a few of them in her defense.

She turned away to go into her office when the sound of the front door opening was followed by a rush of feet and a whispering that seemed to go around the main room as if it were an electrical connection. Whirling around, Susannah braced herself.

Lucas Boyd, with all eyes upon him, walked into the library...again.

Lucas realized, as soon as he entered the building, that he should've chosen someplace a little less public. But he didn't feel right turning up on her doorstep at home. That seemed too personal.

A hell of a thought about the woman he was going to— He broke off his thoughts and approached the front desk.

"Hello, Susannah. I wonder if you'd spare me a few minutes to chat."

She looked all prim and proper today, her hair pulled back in that unflattering bun, a sober dress, though its chocolate color did complement her eyes. He almost believed his coming didn't matter to her, but then he noticed her fingers trembling as she tried to insert a card in a returned book.

"It's a busy time," she muttered, never meeting his gaze.

He scanned the big room. "You folks mind waiting while I talk to Susannah?" After receiving encouraging nods, he returned a triumphant smile to his quarry. "I think everyone will be patient. And what I have to say is kind of important."

Kind of important? He thought what he had to say was earth-shattering. Mind-bending. Cataclysmic.

Without another word, she turned and walked into her office. He followed, his gaze unconsciously enjoying the sway of her hips until he realized what he was doing. He jerked his look back to her bun.

"Look, Lucas, I don't intend to apologize again about what happened yesterday. I may have not...you may not have been pleased, but I had good intentions."

"I'm not here to talk about yesterday...except that I think you owe me for that little trick." He watched the fluctuating color in her cheeks, wanting to touch her, to feel the heat.

"It wasn't that big a deal," she said dismissively, shifting papers around on her desk as if she had business on her mind.

But Lucas wasn't fooled.

With a change of tactics, he said briskly, "You're

right, it wasn't. And it didn't make a hill of beans difference to our situation. If you have your child alone, everyone will still believe it's mine. Both of our reputations will be damaged."

"I'll move."

His heart clutched, and he took a deep breath before he could speak. "That would be a shame. You're well liked here."

She almost turned her back to him, shielding her eyes from his gaze. "Yes, I like it here, too."

"So I have a better solution." He took a step closer, instinctively believing this conversation would be easier if he could touch her. When he reached for her hand, however, she snatched it behind her.

"Wh-what solution?"

This time she faced him squarely, her chin up, ready to do battle. When he'd swept Beth up in plans she didn't vote for, she'd pouted, or tried coyness. Not Susannah. She faced her adversary with every ounce of her, ready to go down for the count.

He swallowed, his throat suddenly dry. It wasn't easy to say those words he'd never thought to utter again. "Marry me." His voice cracked with emotion.

"Wh-what?" she asked faintly. Her face was pale, and he feared she was going to pass out.

"It makes sense, Susannah. I'll get the baby I want, and you will, too. You won't have to worry about supporting it. I'll do that. And I won't have to worry about someone to take care of it." He'd summed it up just like Doc said. But she wasn't impressed. Taking a step back, she gnawed her bottom lip, color returning to her cheeks.

"You shouted at me yesterday for trying to arrange a marriage for you," she reminded him, her gaze fixed on his. "In fact, you assured me marriage was out of the question. You didn't want a wife."

He remembered those words he'd shouted at her. Too bad she did, too. "Uh, I was angry."

"That still doesn't explain your change of mind."

He turned away from her and paced across the small office. "Look, Susannah, those ladies didn't understand. They thought—I mean, you led them to think I was interested in—in a love match." He snuck a look at her, but he couldn't read the expression on her face.

"And you're not. You're just interested in a baby."

He'd known she'd understand if he explained it properly. Sighing with relief, he nodded and offered a smile. "Exactly."

"Thank you for the offer, Mr. Boyd," she said calmly, "but I'm not interested."

Before he could recover, she reached for the door, prepared to end their discussion.

Just as he'd done before, he ordered, "Wait!" Unlike their previous discussion in the office, this time she halted, but she kept her back to him.

"Susannah, think about what you're throwing away. You could have it all…a good home, a family, whatever you need to make you happy." He was pleading for his own happiness, but he didn't think she'd be persuaded by his needs.

"I can have it all without your help, Lucas," she said gently, turning to face him. "I have an appointment Friday with a sperm clinic in Denver."

His heart skipped a beat as he saw his dream escaping. "No!"

"Lucas—I can't discuss this anymore today. My mind—"

"Don't say it! Give me one more chance, Susannah. Let me have one more shot at—at persuading you." He didn't know what he'd come up with that would change her mind, but he wanted some time to think.

"Lucas," she began in protest. "I can't—"

"Yes, you can. This is only Tuesday. Come out to the ranch tomorrow night for dinner. It won't interfere with your schedule for Friday...unless you change your mind. If you do, you can call them Thursday and cancel the appointment." He held his breath while she considered his words.

She lifted her head and stared at him with those big brown eyes that could be warm and laughing, or cold and formal. He couldn't read her answer there.

Drawing in a deep breath, she turned away. "All right."

Her voice was so soft, he wasn't sure he'd heard her answer or had supplied what he wanted to hear. "Did you agree?" he asked, stepping to her side, putting his hand on her shoulder.

"Yes, but I'm warning you. I don't think I'll change my mind. I understand why you want to convince me, but I can have my child without your help, Lucas."

"I know. I know, Susannah," he replied, squeezing her shoulder. "But I appreciate your giving me a chance."

Chapter Six

What did one wear to reject a marriage proposal?

Susannah didn't know the answer to that question as she studied the contents of her closet Wednesday night. Why had she ever agreed to this meeting?

She knew why. It was impossible to look into Lucas's pleading blue eyes, to know the pain he'd suffered and deny him something that would cost her nothing but embarrassment.

Embarrassment that she would suffer when he asked her why she wouldn't marry him. And he would ask. Then she'd have to explain how painful it would be to be married to a man who could only marry her because he had absolutely no interest in her.

And that would be embarrassing because she'd discovered a growing interest in *him.*

He couldn't consider those three blondes she'd set him up with, because they might tempt him from his mourning. After all, whether he admitted it or not, they were all quite like his Beth.

Unlike her.

And, as he'd said several times, he had nothing to give any woman ever again. Not since Beth died.

With a sigh, she pulled out a matching plum blouse and skirt, then searched in her top drawer for a silver concha belt to accent it. She left her hair down for the first time, pulling the sides back with barrettes, the rest curling down her back. Perhaps it was an unconscious attempt to feel prettier, more womanly, in the face of Lucas's businesslike proposal.

Okay, so she was human.

With a shuddering breath, she finished her application of makeup, also an unusual occurrence, and gathered her purse and keys. She was to pick up Abby on her way to Lucas's ranch. After consideration, she'd insisted on Abby's presence, and Lucas had agreed.

"Are you sure you want me to come?" Abby asked as soon as she got in the car.

"Yes, Abby," she replied quietly, softly. Inside, she screamed her need of Abby, a third person, someone who wouldn't be swayed by startling sexual feelings. Someone whose presence would keep Lucas from touching her. Because his touch, even with a friendly intent, made her crazy.

Nothing more was said on the short drive. Lucas's ranch house was located only a couple of miles outside the city limits. Of course, his acreage, large even by Colorado standards, spread out behind the house for miles.

Susannah parked her compact car beside a navy blue Cadillac. "Is that Lucas's car?" Somehow she'd expected a pickup truck.

"No," Abby replied, frowning, "that's Henry Grable's car. Did you know Doc was invited?"

"No. But I suppose it's logical. After all, Dr. Grable started this...I don't know what to call it."

"You know I'm going to support you, whatever you decide, Susannah. But I hope you'll give Lucas's idea some thought. He has a lot to offer a woman."

Susannah bit down on her bottom lip. Maybe she'd made a mistake inviting Abby. It sounded as if Abby was on Lucas's side. "He's—he's not offering what I want."

And she was a fool for even thinking about a real marriage. She didn't think she could make Lucas happy, even if he loved her. Her one venture into a relationship had ended badly, with her fiancé blaming her frigidity for their difficulties. And giving him license to do what he wanted with her best friend.

But she couldn't help the feelings that Lucas Boyd had aroused in her, in spite of her supposed frigidity. As inexperienced as she was, she didn't know how to handle those feelings. And that's why she needed Abby by her side.

The front door to the house opened and Lucas stood silhouetted in the doorway.

With another sigh, Susannah opened her door. "Let's get this over with."

* * *

Lucas heard the sound of a car. His nerves went on alert.

She was here.

His wait would be over. He'd have the answer to his question. Tonight, he'd know if he'd one day soon hold his son in his arms, or whether he'd have to find someone else.

To his surprise, his hands began to shake.

"You okay?" Doc asked, stepping toward him.

"I'm fine. If this—this plan doesn't work out, I'll come up with something else. I *will* have my son."

"'Course you will, Lucas. You almost sound like you don't want Susannah to agree."

"What? Don't be ridiculous," Lucas admonished his friend gruffly. Turning his back on Doc's prying eyes, he walked to the door and opened it.

Doc was wrong, of course. Why would he want her to refuse him when he'd gone to such lengths to persuade her? That was a ridiculous idea.

But one he couldn't deny.

"Evenin', Luke," Abby called out, stepping from the shadows into the porch light.

He returned her greeting, but his gaze searched the darkness for his other guest.

When she finally moved into the light, he stared. With her hair loose and flowing down her shoulders, her body outlined in flattering clothes, she was a far cry from the plain, frumpy librarian he'd first encountered.

Which explained his troubled stomach.

He wanted nothing to do with emotion, with wanting. And yet, in his efforts to convince Susannah, he'd noticed in himself a renewed interest in life, an eagerness to face a new day.

Feelings long dead. Three years long.

They scared him.

"Come in, Abby, Susannah. Welcome to my home."

Even as the two women approached, Lucas drew a deep breath and shored up his determination. It was the hope of his son that was causing the blood to race through his veins once more. Not a woman.

And he was going to win. Susannah was going to agree to give him his son. Because he'd figured out the weak link in her armor.

"I'm glad you could come. Let me show you around the house."

Susannah fell in love.

With the house. Only the house, she assured herself. If she'd planned it herself, she couldn't have been more satisfied.

Oh, not with the decor. It had an air of neglect, of a half-finished project, that reminded her too much of Lucas's past. The furniture was a mixture of sturdy, pioneer furniture, meant to last through the ages, and touches of modern, inexpensive pieces that appeared incongruously beside the rest.

It was a house that needed love to turn it into a home.

You're an idiot, she scolded herself. A sentimental fool. Even worse, she knew Lucas sensed her reaction. If she didn't know better, she'd consider his expression one of gloating.

Abby and Dr. Grable had acted as Lucas's own personal Greek chorus, affirming every advantage he'd pointed out. Financial security. A home. All the time she wanted to care for her child.

"Dinner was delicious," she said politely as she wiped her lips with her napkin.

"I'll tell Frankie you appreciated it. He's a good cook."

"Yes, excellent," Abby hurriedly agreed. "He'll be a big help. Most new mothers don't have enough help." She elbowed the good doctor as if she feared he'd forget his role.

"Absolutely," he hurriedly agreed, putting down his fork. "Most new mothers have to do too much too soon. Frankie will be a big help."

Susannah tried to hide her smile as the doctor looked longingly at his last bite of coconut custard pie. Keeping his eye on Abby, he slowly picked up his fork. Then, with his prize in hand, he hurried it to his mouth.

"I think Frankie would make it hard to regain my figure, don't you, Doctor? That pie was impossible to resist."

"It was mighty good," he agreed with a grin that disappeared as Abby elbowed him again. "I mean—um, I'm sure Frankie has some low calorie recipes."

Several remarks about the likelihood of a man cooking for a bunch of hardworking cowboys even thinking of calories passed through Susannah's head, but she said nothing.

What was the point? In spite of all the advantages on display, Frankie included, she couldn't accept Lucas's offer. She would pay the price of a loveless marriage, daily rejection of the feelings she might develop.

Work had never bothered her. Coldness. Loneliness. Those were her fears. And even among the crowd of people on Lucas's ranch, she would be lonely.

The object of her thoughts, her host, settled back in his chair at the head of the table. "Well, Susannah, have you thought about my idea? Have we convinced you?"

Something in his look, his tone, made her leery. She'd earlier thought she'd detected a self-congratulatory smirk, but something was different now.

"No, Lucas, I'm sorry. I still have to refuse your—your gracious offer."

It took some courage to meet his gaze, but she did, hoping she hid the turmoil inside her. Instead of looking disappointed, he regarded her steadily, seriously.

"So, the idea of wealth and comfort didn't move you?"

She swallowed, her throat suddenly dry. "No, thank you."

"You have beautiful manners, Susannah."

His non sequitur puzzled her. She looked at Abby and the doctor to see if they understood his meaning, but they looked as nonplussed as she felt.

"I bet your mother was from the South."

She nodded hesitantly, then said, "From Texas."

"Ah. But your parents are both dead, aren't they?"

"Yes."

"No extended family, cousins, aunts and uncles?"

Growing more and more uneasy, Susannah shook her head, confirming his words.

He leaned forward, staring at her intently, "What will happen to your baby if you fall ill? Or, God forbid, die in a car wreck?"

She closed her eyes even as she heard Abby gasp. She wanted to hide the pain that filled her.

"Lucas Boyd, shame on you!" Abby protested.

Even the doctor protested. "That's hard, Lucas."

"No, it's the truth. While Susannah may not need my wealth, my home, her baby does. If he's my son, I'll be there for him if she can't. And she knows I'll love him. If something happens to me, she'll have the financial means to carry on. But—" he paused, but Susannah didn't open her eyes "—if she has her child alone, he could end up in a foster home, if something should happen to her."

She prayed she'd open her eyes and discover she'd been having a bad dream. That she was home in her solitary bed. That she'd never met Lucas Boyd.

"Is that what you want, Susannah?"

That low, almost whispered question echoed in her heart. She opened her eyes and stared at her tormentor. Her bottom lip trembled as she tried to speak, to respond to his question.

She couldn't.

"Oh, my poor dear," Abby moaned and leaped up to come around the table to her side.

"Boy, I think you may have gone too far," Dr. Grable protested, standing also.

Lucas remained seated. "I didn't mean to hurt you, Susannah. I just wanted to make you think about what's best for the baby. Our baby."

Chills coursed through her body. She wanted to get up and race out of his house, away from his words. But she didn't think her legs would hold her.

Finally she composed herself enough to whisper to Abby, "I want to go home."

"Of course you do, dear. Come on. We'll get away from these nasty men," Abby agreed, taking Susannah's arm to help her up.

"Hey, I didn't do anything," Dr. Grable protested.

Now Lucas stood. "You promised you'd answer my question tonight," he reminded her, again drawing Abby's ire.

"Haven't you done enough?" Abby demanded. "The poor girl is shaking like a leaf."

"Please, Abby, let's just go," Susannah insisted as she tried to pull herself together. "My answer—"

"Never mind," the cowboy abruptly said, cutting her off. "Think about what I said. Tell me tomorrow."

She wanted to scream no at him. But she couldn't. The reason his question had shaken her so was that he'd found her Achilles' heel. He'd struck at the one weakness to her plan.

If she had a child, it would be totally dependent on her.

So now she was faced with her selfishness, or giving up her hope of having a child.

Or marrying Lucas Boyd.

Lucas felt like a wolf that had savaged an innocent lamb. The stricken look on Susannah's face as she'd hurried from his house, quite possibly from his life, would stay with him for a long time.

His secret weapon had certainly shaken her, he admitted as he paced the bedroom floor. He'd been right. He'd discovered her weakness. After he'd seen her tender heart, seeing how much she worried about hurting even him, he'd known she would never be able to deny her child.

But he'd found himself shaken, too. The urge to beat Abby to her side, to sweep her into his arms and promise never to hurt her again, had almost paralyzed him.

It was because he'd felt responsible. Felt, hell! He *was* responsible. His daddy had always taught him to protect women, to care for them. Instead he'd hurt her.

That was the only reason he'd reacted so powerfully. He'd done something his daddy wouldn't have approved of. It had nothing to do with Susannah.

But he'd repeat it a thousand times if it would bring him his son.

He paced across the room again.

For Colorado in the fall, it was a mild night. But Susannah shivered beneath the blankets on her bed.

Lucas Boyd had forced her to face facts. Her child, if she had a child by artificial insemination, would be totally dependent on her. If something happened to her, the baby would go into foster care, as Lucas had said.

Could she take that risk? Could she selfishly give life to a child so she wouldn't be alone, knowing that if she died, the child would face the same difficulty?

But could she give up her unborn child?

She rubbed her hand over her flat stomach as if a child were already growing there. She'd longed for this child, prayed for it, planned for its care. Loved it.

Tossing and turning, she debated her options until early in the frosty morning. Finally she fell asleep without coming to a decision.

But when she woke, the questions were waiting, lurking in the shadows. What would she choose?

"Dang it! What's wrong with you today?" Frankie asked as his boss paced through the kitchen for the fourth time that morning. "I kin hardly make one pass with the mop before you muddy the floor again."

"What?" Lucas asked, staring at Frankie with a bewildered look on his face.

"Never mind. Just get along."

Lucas rubbed his forehead, unsure where he was heading when Frankie interrupted him. He couldn't concentrate on anything this morning…other than Susannah's decision. He'd stopped her last night because he thought she needed time for his argument to sink in.

But he didn't understand why. He was offering her everything she could want.

Except himself.

And she had no more interest in that kind of relationship than he did. If she did, she wouldn't be considering a test tube in Denver.

The phone rang and he almost leaped across the kitchen to the extension on the wall. "Hello?"

"Luke? This is Mike. I noticed some fencing down on your western boundary, just below Culligan's Pass. Thought you'd want to know."

"Oh. Thanks, Mike. I'll send a couple of the boys over right away." His heart rate settled back to normal.

"Maybe you should go, yourself," Frankie suggested, as Lucas got off the phone.

Lucas frowned at him. "Me? Why?"

"To get you out of my kitchen," Frankie said with exasperation, leaning on his mop.

"I'm going to town," Lucas abruptly said. He'd borne the suspense long enough.

"You comin' back for lunch?"

"No." If Susannah agreed, he'd take her to lunch. If not...well, he wouldn't have an appetite.

"Yes, I understand. I'm sorry for the inconvenience," Susannah said with a shaky voice. She put down the receiver and covered her face with trembling fingers.

"What inconvenience?"

Her head whipped up, and she stared at Lucas Boyd, who was leaning against the doorjamb to her small office. She'd hoped for some time to compose herself before she had to face him. Time to let her raw emotions retreat, find protective cover.

"What inconvenience?" he asked again, staring at her with passionate eyes.

"My canceling the appointment with the sperm bank." She didn't offer any explanation.

A spark of hope fired up in his gaze. "Because?"

No patient waiting on his part. Lucas Boyd wanted his trophy at once.

"Because I realized you were right. I couldn't have a child alone, with no safety net in case—no one to care for my child."

He left the doorjamb and sauntered closer. She knew it was her imagination at fault, but his movement seemed like that of an animal closing in for the kill.

"I'd make a great safety net, Susannah."

Her chin lifted. She wanted to deny his words, to tell him she'd found another way. A way that wouldn't involve putting her heart, her soul, at risk.

But she hadn't.

Slowly she looked down at the pile of papers on her desk. "I know."

He stepped closer and lifted her chin with his big, callused hand. "Tell me, Susannah. Spell it out plain and clear. Are you going to marry me, have my baby?"

Moisture filled her eyes, but she wasn't a coward. Meeting his stare, she nodded.

His reaction only underlined their future together. He released her chin as if she'd burned his fingers, and he took a step backward.

"Have you changed your mind?" she asked, her voice shaking. Was she failing again at a relationship before it had even begun? Had he already realized she wasn't…wasn't good with the physical side of love?

"No!" he protested hoarsely. "No, I haven't changed my mind. But I've been afraid I couldn't convince you. It's just taking me a little time to figure out that I've won."

"Won? You make it sound like a game, a challenge. We're talking about a life, a—a child."

"I know that! Damn it, I know that better than anyone. I stood there and watched my baby boy die," he shouted, suddenly pacing her little office. "Don't try to tell me what we're talking about!"

The deep breath Susannah drew shuddered its way through her. Had she made a mistake? Could she handle close quarters with this man, with his past, his pain, his memories?

"Sorry," he apologized even as she worried. "I—I'm thrilled with your decision, Susannah. But it's a lot to adjust to. Even though we talked about it before, it—it seems more real now."

"You can still change your mind."

A smile slowly grew on his firm lips, reaching his eyes. "No, sweetheart. I'm not going to change my mind. I'm going to be a daddy. I couldn't be happier."

She looked away. Too much exposure to his happiness would damage her heart for sure.

"Come on. Let me take you to lunch to celebrate," he said, moving toward her again.

She pressed against the back of her chair. "But everyone would see us."

"That's okay. We're going to be married. They might as well get used to the idea." Without leaving her any choice in the matter, he seized her hand and pulled her from her chair. "Hurry up. Suddenly I'm starving."

Susannah spent her energy trying to get her feet underneath her before she fell on her face. Which made it impossible to protest his action until they were out the door and in the main room of the library.

"Lucas, please—"

"You don't want to go eat?" he asked, frowning, coming to an abrupt halt.

"It's not... Lunch isn't necessary."

One eyebrow slid up over his sparkling eyes. "Sweetheart, it's sure necessary where I come from. Don't you eat?"

"I mean you don't have to buy me lunch."

He blinked at her, as if he didn't understand her words. Then, a trifle grimly, he muttered, "I think the occasion warrants it."

Without any more conversation, he led her across the street to The Red Slipper.

She didn't want to go in, but with Lucas's hand gripping her arm, Susannah didn't think she had a choice. It seemed to her, as they stepped through the door, that the entire room grew still, silent, watching.

Her cheeks heated up and she discovered a strange urge to hide her face against Luke's strong shoulder. Great! Nothing would confirm the gossip faster.

Lucas seemed at ease. "Morning, Molly. We need a table for two."

The hostess grinned. "You cuttin' down, Luke? Last time you had three ladies waiting for you."

"Yeah, I'm cutting down. Permanently." He added a big grin, and conversation picked up at once, everyone abuzz with this latest tidbit of gossip.

"Lucas!" Susannah protested hoarsely.

He buried his nose in her hair and whispered, "You can't keep secrets in this town. And I won't have anyone thinking I'm ashamed of my baby's mother."

Stunned, unable to move as fast to acceptance as he, Susannah stared.

"Sit down," he said gently, as if realizing her difficulty.

She flopped into a chair, aware of Molly's stare. When the hostess handed her the menu, she buried her face behind it.

"Enjoy your meal."

"We will," Lucas said.

Susannah peeped over the top of her menu to find him smiling. "You're enjoying this, aren't you?"

He settled in his chair before he answered. The smile left his face and he shrugged. "We're both going to achieve our dream. What's not to enjoy?"

With a jerky nod of agreement, she returned to the menu. When the waitress arrived at their table, an old friend of Lucas's, of course, Susannah was able to order her lunch without stumbling.

Maybe she could get through this...this arrangement. What was important was the baby, her child.

Their child.

"Lucas, you do realize the baby could be a girl, don't you?" She'd meant to mention that possibility before now.

The grin returned to his face. "Not a chance. Boyds have boys."

As if she were talking to herself, she said, "I was hoping for a girl."

He reached across the table to take her hand. "Maybe we can have more than one. Surely there have been some girls somewhere in my family tree."

She gasped, staring at him. How had he known? Had he realized how much she hated the idea of having an only child? Like herself? Or was it a lucky guess?

He seemed to recognize her surprise. "Sorry, Susannah. I know we haven't talked about more children, but I'm not against the idea. Are you?"

"No."

"So, we need to set the date. Can you be ready by next Saturday?"

Before she could answer, the waitress set their plates in front of them, giving Susannah a breathing space.

"Next Saturday?" she repeated after they were alone.

"Yeah. I'll talk to the pastor, and we can get a license."

"I thought we should wait until—until after I'm pregnant before we actually marry."

Chapter Seven

Lucas shook his head, wondering if he'd heard correctly. What was wrong with the woman? He offered marriage and she suggested an affair?

"Why?"

She didn't meet his gaze. "It makes sense. The purpose of our marriage is to have a child. If I can't get pregnant, we'd both feel foolish, wouldn't we?"

"Is there any reason you can't get pregnant? Did Doc find something when he examined you?" He watched her closely, wondering what was going on.

"No. He said everything was fine."

"Then we'll go ahead and marry. I want my son conceived *after* the wedding, not before." Feeling he'd settled the matter, he turned his attention to the food in front of him. Not that he was as calm as he hoped he looked. But he didn't want Susannah to know about the jitters in his stomach.

She didn't respond. When she picked up her fork

to begin her meal also, he relaxed somewhat. Before she ate anything, however, she lowered her fork to her plate.

"Maybe you should go ahead and…and give Doc some, uh, some specimens. That way we can get the process started as soon as possible. I'll—"

"I should do what?" His voice was low, almost guttural, but if he'd understood what she said, no one would blame him. He waited for her explanation.

"I know you said you wanted us to be married, but surely, a couple of days won't—"

"What does Doc have to do with anything?"

That blasted bottom lip of hers was trembling. The urge to comfort, to touch, to kiss—nope, he didn't really want to do those things. It was her distress, not her sex appeal, that moved him. Wasn't it?

"Dr. Grable will perform the procedure."

A coldness settled around his heart. Leaning forward, he said, "Lady, the only one performing will be me, and I promise you won't call it a 'procedure,' like canning tomatoes, when we're finished."

He watched her cheeks flash fire and then go deathly pale. Clamping her lips tightly together, she didn't say a word as she hurried from the table in the direction of the ladies' room.

What in the hell was going on? She thought they'd marry and not have sex? Had he missed something here? Knowing he couldn't enter the ladies' room, he summoned the waitress to the table.

"Something wrong with the special?" she asked, looking at his plate.

"No, but Susannah left the table in a hurry. Would you check the rest room to see if she's okay?"

"You think the food made her sick?"

"No, she hasn't eaten anything. Just check on her for me." Right after he'd spoken the words, Susannah reappeared. Both Lucas and the waitress watched her progress back to the table.

"You okay, hon?" the waitress asked, studying her.

"I'm fine."

"Your boyfriend here thought you were sick. Maybe you're pregnant," she suggested with a chuckle.

Lucas glared at her and, if possible, Susannah turned even more pale.

As if suddenly realizing her teasing had gone awry, the waitress hurriedly apologized and dashed off to another table.

"Susannah, what's going on here?"

"Nothing," she whispered. Since she picked up her fork and took a bite of the meat loaf she'd ordered, Lucas ate, too, but he couldn't shake the feeling that something was wrong.

"Are you sure you're healthy?"

Woodenly, without looking at him, she replied, "Do you want Dr. Grable to write out a certificate of health for me?"

"No, I didn't mean—"

"It's all right, Lucas. I understand what is at stake, what kind of commodity I'm offering. If I can't produce a child, I realize—"

"Damn it! Stop it, Susannah. You make it sound like we're bartering pigs for chickens, here."

For the first time since their arrival at the café, her gaze met his. "We are. I'm trading a part of my child for the security you've promised. You're trading a promise to love and protect in return. Love and protect the child, I mean," she added hurriedly, embarrassed again.

Why did something feel wrong? He frowned. "I will protect you as well, Susannah. After all, you'll be my wife."

She straightened her spine and replied crisply, as if she was once more in control of herself, "I can take care of myself, Lucas. All I'm asking is that you keep your word to our child. And I know you will do that."

"I promise, Susannah."

She nodded and took another bite. They finished the rest of their meal in silence. She left at least half of the meat loaf and vegetables on her plate. It took effort to control the urge to press her to finish her meal. But he managed.

As soon as he'd eaten the last bite of his food, she said, "I need to return to work, Lucas. I have a lot of things to do."

He frowned again. She seemed extremely anxious to get away from him. "Okay, but we're decided on next Saturday?" At her nod, he said, "I'll call the preacher and see if the church is available. And I'll bear the cost of the wedding. After all—"

"No! That's my responsibility. Besides, it won't

cost all that much. There'll just be my dress…and—and a ring for you. Do you mind wearing a ring?"

He considered his response. Oh, not about the ring. Of course he intended to wear a ring. But if she thought they were going to be married secretly, as if he were ashamed of her, she had another thought coming. "I'll be glad to wear a ring. We can go into the Springs Monday and pick something out. And you can shop for a gown there. I'll take care of everything else."

"What else?" she asked with a frown, pausing in her movement to leave.

"A few minor details. Don't worry about it." He stood and came around the table as she shoved back her chair.

"But I want to—"

He stopped her words with a kiss. He'd intended it to be light, a notice served to the community of his intentions. But that damn lower lip, both lips in fact, were soft, surprised and downright inviting. Even the slightest physical contact between them seemed to arouse in him long-dormant sensations. She made him aware of his masculinity as no other woman did.

When he finally lifted his head, she stared at him with tragic eyes, as if he'd just broken her heart. "What? It was only a kiss, Susannah. What's wrong?"

"Nothing," she said hurriedly, ducking her head and turning away. "I have to get back to the library."

He let her go alone. That seemed to be what she

wanted. But he was puzzled...and worried. Why should his kiss upset her? Did she think they wouldn't touch just because they weren't marrying for love?

If that was her idea, it was a good thing he'd kissed her. He might not love her, and have no intention of loving her, but a man has needs. And he'd just discovered one of his most urgent needs was kissing Susannah.

Susannah felt like a mouse scurrying back to her hole after the big, ferocious cat had pawed her. Lucas Boyd was dangerous. Not because he would ever intentionally hurt her, but because his careless touch could destroy her.

She'd thought he understood that touching, sex, lovemaking, wouldn't be a part of their marriage. When he'd dismissed Dr. Grable as a part of their pregnancy plan, she'd known she was in trouble.

When her fiancé had condemned her as frigid, she hadn't argued. After all, she had felt no urge, no heat, no impatience for her wedding bed. He'd blamed her for his affair with her friend.

Books were Susannah's living. She'd read enough self-help books to know she was not to blame for his behavior. But her lack of interest in sex with him, the distance she felt when he touched her, had coincided with his condemnation.

She wished she could feel as distant when Lucas kissed her.

He wasn't being dishonest with her. No, he'd told

her up-front that there was nothing personal about his interest in her. He wanted a baby.

The old-fashioned way.

Impossible to do without touching. And Susannah was finding it difficult to deal with her response when he touched her. When his lips met hers, she lost all rational thought. But he brought her to earth with a *thunk* when his words underlined his concept of their marriage.

They had only shared one kiss and she was already out of control. How was she going to protect herself? How was she going to hide her response?

The last thing she wanted was for him to feel sorry for her, to realize how needy she was. They couldn't live together, coexist, if that happened. He'd be embarrassed and disinterested. She'd be miserable.

The only comfort she could find was that it was one of the busiest days at the library. Once she entered the building, her work pulled at her, tugging her thoughts from the disaster of her personal life.

At least she would have her work, giving her an air of normalcy during the day.

At night, she was in big trouble.

"Doc, did you examine Susannah when she first visited you?" Lucas asked over the phone.

"Of course I did. Why?"

"Did she discuss any, uh, her past?"

"No. Didn't say much. What's the problem, boy? Did she turn you down?"

"No, she agreed."

"Hallelujah! When?"

"Next Saturday. Will you stand up with me?"

"I'd be delighted."

"When she agreed, she thought we should wait until after she got pregnant to get married. I thought maybe she was afraid she couldn't, you know, conceive." Lucas wrapped the telephone cord tightly around one finger, watching it grow pale as the blood flow was cut off.

"I didn't see a problem. She's very healthy."

Lucas unwrapped his finger and let out a sigh. "Okay. Well, I've talked to the preacher and the wedding's set for four o'clock next Saturday. We'll have the reception here afterward. Pass the word along, will you?"

"The entire town?"

"Every last one of them. We're going to celebrate."

Susannah waited until she got home that evening to call Abby. Though they weren't having a formal wedding, she'd need someone to stand up for her, and she wanted Abby.

"Abby? It's Susannah. I wondered if—"

"It's about time you called. You are going to ask me to stand up for you, aren't you?" Without waiting for Susannah to speak, she continued, "A'course, I'll understand if you want someone younger, but—"

"Of course I want you to stand up for me. But how did you know?"

"Lord'a'mercy, child, it's all over town."

"You mean Lucas's behavior in the café?"

"Aw, he's kissed women before. But the wedding

is the big news. We've got lots to do before then. Mark next Thursday evening off your schedule. That's when we're giving you a shower. And Friday night you'll spend here with me. Since the wedding's at four, we'll—"

"What? The wedding's when?" Susannah couldn't believe it. The entire town knew when her wedding was scheduled before she did?

"At four. With a big party at the ranch afterward for the entire town. There'll be a big cake, lots of food and Jed Roy is over the moon with the order for flowers. Didn't Lucas tell you?"

"I have to go, Abby. I'll call you later." Even though Abby was still protesting when she hung up the receiver, Susannah didn't hesitate. This might not be a real marriage, but Lucas Boyd had another thought coming if he thought he could run roughshod over her.

Rage filled her as she marched out of her little house to her car. She only hoped her rage wouldn't disappear by the time she reached his ranch, because she knew she'd need its energy to deal with the ornery man who *thought* he was about to become her husband!

To her relief, her anger was still simmering when she jerked to a stop in front of his house. By the time she reached the door, she'd stoked it with the reminder of how little she figured into his plans.

Only her baby.

After her knock he opened the door with a smile. "Susannah, I just tried to call you."

How dare he? He acted as if he was pleased to see

her. The pain was so acute, her prepared speech went out the window. Without warning, she slapped him. "The wedding's off!"

Then she ran.

He caught her before she reached her car.

"What the hell's gotten into you, woman?"

She couldn't answer him. Tears filled her eyes and she was choked up. All she wanted was to get away, to hide in the dark until the panic eased.

In spite of her pushing and pulling, she couldn't get away. He held her tight. He even tried to force her face up, so he could see, but that at least she could prevent. Finally, in a surprise move, he threw her over one of his broad shoulders and headed for the house.

"Put me down! I want to leave!" She choked out the words, flailing uselessly at his back.

"Not until you explain," he said, his voice grim with determination.

"All right, put me down. I'll explain," she assured him with almost gleeful anger. She was glad she had an excuse to break off their six-hour engagement.

Because she was afraid.

With a sigh, she hung limply, no longer struggling. She was afraid. It hurt to admit her cowardice, but that was why she had become so enraged.

He opened the door and stepped inside, into the light, just as Frankie entered the hallway.

"Uh, everything okay, boss?"

"Yeah, Frankie. There'll be one more for dinner. Okay?"

"Sure, boss. There's plenty of food." Then he

scurried back down the hall and into the kitchen as Lucas let Susannah slide down his body to stand beside him.

Susannah closed her eyes. Could she embarrass herself more? Probably her behavior would be fodder for the gossip chain that existed in the small town before breakfast the next morning.

"What happened?" he asked.

She opened her eyes, suddenly weary. And heartbroken. "It doesn't matter. It's over. I never should've agreed."

Dully she tried to move around him, to walk away.

Catching her shoulders in his strong hands, he held her firm. "Come on, Susannah, tell me what made you mad, made you change your mind."

"Why ask me? Probably within the hour the tomtoms will be beating across the mountains, detailing our argument, just as they detailed our wedding. You can wait until then to find out." She knew she was being unfair but she was desperate.

"What are you talking about? You're not making any sense."

"No, I'm not. I'm being overly sensitive, melodramatic, demanding, expecting to be consulted about our wedding before the entire town is informed. It's a good thing you discovered I'm outrageous before you actually married me." She kept her spine straight, her shoulders back. But she couldn't look him in the eye.

Finally she raised her gaze. The silence had gone on too long. Why didn't he say anything?

* * *

Lucas was too busy cursing his insensitivity.

When he'd married Beth, he remembered the weeks before the marriage, the details that consumed her, the way she'd gotten irritated with him because he didn't care about what color the bridesmaids' gowns were going to be.

Why had he thought Susannah wouldn't care? She was a woman, and this marriage would be her only opportunity to indulge in sentimentality.

No wonder she'd gotten angry.

"I'm sorry, Susannah. I should've called you and told you the only possible time was four o'clock next Saturday. But since it was the only time the preacher could make it, I assumed it would be all right with you."

His apology didn't solve anything.

She tugged futilely on his hold. "Please, let's just forget it. We've made a mistake."

"No, we haven't. *I* made a mistake. I was insensitive. But there's no need to call off the wedding. Our reason is still valid." He ducked his head, trying to see her face. "Susannah?"

She kept her head lowered, but tears trailed down her pale cheeks. "Please, let me go," she whispered.

"I can't." Without thought, he wrapped his arms around her, pulling her against him. "You're going to take away my dream because I didn't think? I promise I won't do it again."

Almost as if in slow motion, she laid her head on his shoulder, her face buried in his neck, letting her body rest against his.

His reaction boded well for their marriage bed.

Even as his manhood swelled and surged, his lips sought hers, his hands stroked and coaxed her participation. When her arms slid around his neck, her fingers weaving through his hair, along his neck, her mouth opened to him, he thought he was going to lose control and embarrass himself right there.

Not that he stopped, or let her go. In fact, he pressed her tighter against him, loving the feel of her breasts' tight buds rubbing against his chest. He deepened the kiss, pushing his tongue past any barriers, encouraging her to join him.

And she did.

When one of his hands sank to the front of her blouse and began unfastening the buttons, she returned the favor, pulling his shirt aside and stroking his chest.

He let his lips leave hers, seeking new treasures, but he couldn't stay away from their luscious softness. His hand cupped a neglected breast as his mouth plundered hers again. He thought he'd eat her alive. And still be hungry for her again.

He'd never felt this way before.

Not even with Beth.

Such a betrayal jolted him out of his sensual haze, and he stumbled back, shocked.

He didn't have long to dwell on the traitorous thought, however, because Susannah turned and ran again.

"No!" he yelled even as he caught her.

The kitchen door swung open almost simultaneously and Frankie opened his mouth to announce dinner. "Dinner is— Uh, sorry." He hastily retreated.

"We'll be right there," Lucas called out.

Then he turned his attention to the mass of nerves in his arms. Even as she buttoned up her blouse, she was trembling like a leaf.

"He didn't see anything, sweetheart. There's nothing to be embarrassed about."

He supposed he could count it a good thing that she looked him in the eye. Except for that glow of anger.

"I can't stay to eat. I have to leave."

"Come on, Frankie's already fixed everything. It will give us a chance to talk."

"In front of Frankie?" she asked, scandalized.

"No. I'll, um, I'll suggest he eat in the bunkhouse tonight. He won't mind."

"No, I have to go."

"Susannah, I'm not letting you go until we work out our problems. I'm not giving up my dream."

She went completely still in his hold, and he feared he'd said the wrong thing. To his surprise, however, she drew a deep breath and stopped pulling away. "No. I guess not."

Without another word to him, she finished buttoning her blouse, tucked it into her skirt, smoothed back her hair, caught in its usual bun and turned to walk to the kitchen.

"Susannah—" he called out and she turned to stare at him.

"Didn't you want to eat?"

Hell, yes, he wanted to eat. He'd had a busy day.

But his head was all ajumble. He didn't want her to
leave. He didn't want her to stay. How could he face
what had popped into his mind when she was still
there?

Still tempting him.

What was he going to do?

Chapter Eight

Her wedding day.

Susannah lay in Abby's guest room bed, staring at the ceiling. Abby had ordered her not to get up before ten this morning…8:47 and counting.

She should be exhausted. There had been a hundred chores to accomplish before her wedding. Including packing. She'd considered keeping her little house, but coward that she was, she couldn't face either Abby's or Lucas's reaction.

She and her fiancé had come to a silent agreement at their last meeting. They would stay as far apart as possible until the ceremony. At least, Susannah assumed that was what Lucas wanted since he'd avoided being alone with her.

She knew it was her preference.

In fact, she was surprised that Lucas was willing to go ahead with the ceremony. Especially since she'd already revealed how inadequate she was in...in certain areas. The expression on his face when he'd pushed his way out of her arms had confirmed her worst fears.

The click of the door snapped her from her thoughts. Surprisingly she almost chuckled to see Abby's kind face peeking through a narrow slit between the door and the wall.

"Come in, Abby, and give me permission to get up. I'm tired of lying here."

"Land's sake, child. You were supposed to sleep late this morning."

"But I always get up by seven, Abby. It's habit. I did sleep until almost eight this morning. Will that do?"

"Why, of course, child. I was going to serve you breakfast in bed. But you can come to the table if you want."

"I want," she replied succinctly and shoved back the covers. "I've never been much for eating in bed."

She slipped on a robe and followed Abby to the kitchen. Her day had begun.

He'd been up since before sunrise.

What in hell was he doing? He couldn't marry again. If he did, he'd face the pain of loss, as he'd lost Beth and his little boy.

He'd thought he could protect his heart by not loving a woman. But his child? Didn't he intend to love his child? He'd promised Susannah he would. Of course he would. He couldn't help himself.

And the fear of losing that child, as he'd lost his first child, scared him to death.

After hours of pacing, he knew he couldn't give up the hope of a son. But he'd gird his heart, keep it locked away, until that child lived and breathed in front of him. Until he could hear its heartbeat, watch it take a breath of sweet air.

Lucas drew a shuddering breath. He'd hold his unborn child at a distance as he intended to hold his wife at a distance.

Except for making love to her.

Having sex.

"Boss, breakfast's ready," Frankie called up the stairs.

As if escaping from a torture chamber, Lucas rushed out of his bedroom and down the stairs to the kitchen.

When Doc arrived that afternoon to escort him to the church, Lucas had put on his best suit, a crisp white shirt and a silver-and-blue tie. His mirror told him he looked the part of the eager groom.

Except for the pallor beneath his tan.

"Ready, boy?"

"Am I making a mistake, Doc?" He wanted to grab the older man by the neck. It was his fault, after all.

"No, Lucas, you're not making a mistake. It's time for you to enter the human race again."

Lucas stared at him, afraid he was right.

"Come on. It's too late now." Doc took him by the arm and led him out to his Cadillac.

Doc remained at his side as he entered the church

where he'd married his sweet Beth. She'd looked like a delicate doll in her white gown, all innocence and eagerness.

It took all his courage to face the filled church. But, with Doc at his side, he walked down the aisle to greet Pastor Collier who was waiting at the altar. The people quieted and the pastor signaled the organist to begin to play.

Though he'd organized most of the wedding and all of the reception at his ranch, Lucas had meticulously informed Susannah of each event, giving her every choice, during the week. He didn't want a repeat of the night she'd heard of his plans secondhand. But he'd consulted with her from a distance. He hadn't seen her since their confrontation.

Since neither he nor Susannah had parents, the only person to precede his bride down the aisle was Abby. When the organ music swelled and the guests stood and faced the front of the church, Lucas closed his eyes, unwilling to face his future.

He hadn't seen Susannah's gown. He'd given Abby strict instructions and she'd promised to keep Susannah from choosing a sensible suit. Even though their marriage wasn't romantic, he felt he owed her a real wedding.

A murmur ran through the audience and he snapped open his eyes. And understood why she'd gained their attention. She wore a white satin gown that draped her tall, rounded figure, sweeping the floor. The white drifting veil gave her a fairy princess air, only heightened by her brunette curls touching her shoulders.

He drew a deep breath. *You don't care about her. You don't care about her. You're just going to make love to her. That's all.*

Susannah's hands trembled as they clutched the huge bouquet of pale pink rosebuds and baby's breath Lucas had sent her. In spite of the distance they'd maintained this week, he had gone the extra mile to provide a beautiful wedding.

She was grateful. Really she was. But she was so worried over what would happen after the reception that she could scarcely concentrate.

Raising her eyes, she stared at the tall, handsome man waiting for her. Soon to be her husband. When she reached his side, she lowered her gaze to her trembling flowers and waited.

The music stopped and the minister began the ceremony.

They should've discussed the vows, she realized as Lucas repeated the words. He was promising to love her and she knew his words were a lie. Again she looked at him, but his gaze was fixed on the minister.

Then it was her turn. Like Lucas, she mouthed the words, knowing that in her heart she was promising no such thing. Not that she hated him. But she wasn't promising to love him. It was too frightening. Her gaze flashed to his, panic filling it.

He frowned and squeezed her hand, as if to offer support.

She turned back to the minister and Abby handed her the gold band she'd purchased for Lucas. Dr.

Grable did the same for Lucas. When he slid a ring on her trembling finger, she started, surprised by the diamonds. She'd tried on a plain gold band on Monday. Now she was wearing at least three carats of diamonds—an incredibly beautiful ring.

After Lucas had received his ring, the minister informed them they were now man and wife and added the words she'd been dreading. "You may kiss the bride."

Lucas lifted the veil, then drew her into his arms and lowered his mouth to hers. Every time he'd kissed her, she'd lost control, her body responding to his touch no matter how much she'd intended to remain distant. This kiss was no exception.

"Ahem. Mr. and Mrs. Boyd, I think we're ready for the reception," the minister said, breaking into the passion they were sharing.

Susannah's cheeks flamed as Lucas turned her toward the doors of the church and the crowd cheered, some of them laughing, she supposed, at the length of the kiss.

"Ready?" Lucas whispered, his arm around her waist.

She nodded, though she had no idea what she was agreeing to. She was still lost in a haze of passion. How could she respond to Lucas that way when no other man had ever aroused her?

Lucas took his arm from around her and laced his fingers with hers, pulling her from the altar down the aisle. A lot of well-wishers patted them on the shoulder or stopped them for a handshake as they made their way out of the church.

"Looks like everyone made it," Lucas whispered when they stepped outside in the late-afternoon sunshine. "We'll have a full house at the ranch. There hasn't been a party there since…I mean—there'll be a crowd."

"I haven't helped prepare anything," she returned, feeling guilty.

"No problem. Half the town has dropped off food and Frankie's been cooking for three days. We'll have leftovers into next week."

How mundane to be discussing leftovers after leaving the church. If she could hold on to such practical things, maybe she'd be able to handle this liaison better than she thought.

Doc and Abby stepped out after them. "Let's get a move on," Doc ordered. "We're going to be surrounded in ten seconds."

His Cadillac was waiting by the door and Lucas helped Susannah get her gown into the back seat and then slid in after her. Abby joined Doc in the front.

They were back at the ranch in five minutes, not enough time to worry about conversation. Halfway there, however, Lucas realized he was still holding Susannah's hand and jerked his away, as if she'd been trying to trap him.

She missed the warmth of his touch. But she wasn't surprised.

"All right, now," Abby said over her shoulder. "You two stand by the front door so you can greet everyone. I'll check on Frankie. He was in the back of the church and scooted out just ahead of you."

For the next hour, Susannah greeted everyone

she'd ever met, and a few strangers, too, as Mrs. Lucas Boyd. It was a strange experience. And draining. When she sagged against Lucas briefly, he immediately called a halt to the line.

"My wife needs to eat something. Did you skip lunch?" he demanded.

Susannah couldn't believe he sounded as if he were her keeper, not her husband. "I ate something."

"What?"

Her mind was buzzing with the day's events. "I don't remember. I'm fine."

Ignoring her protest, he pulled her into the living room and found her a place on the sofa. "I'll bring you some food."

"No, I can—" She didn't finish her protest because he'd disappeared. "Well, really!"

"Let him wait on you, honey. It won't last long," one older lady assured her, laughing.

"True," another chimed in. "When I was pregnant with our first baby, Walter waited on me hand and foot. By the time the third came along, he'd plop down in a chair and ask me to wait on him."

Several other ladies had stories to tell, and Susannah relaxed for the first time that day. And felt more married than she had up till then.

Lucas returned with a plate piled high. "Eat quickly. We need to cut the wedding cake in a few minutes," he warned. "Do you need anything else?" He set a cup of coffee beside her.

"No, I'm fine."

"Go on, Luke, go out to the barn and man-talk. We're taking care of everything here."

He walked away and Susannah looked at the woman who'd spoken. "The barn?"

"At these parties, the men always end up in the barn, having some beers and talking about sports or cows or something else we don't care about."

"Oh. But the cake—"

"There's no rush. Eat up. You'll need your strength for tonight. That boy's all man."

Her ribald comment brought the blood to Susannah's cheeks again, and she tucked into her food. She didn't want to think about tonight, after everyone left. But the image of Lucas, all two hundred hunky pounds of him, was uppermost in her mind.

Abby came over. "Want to remove your veil? Is it bothering you?"

"Yes, thank you, Abby." She hadn't intended to have a veil but according to Abby, Lucas insisted. In fact, she'd intended to buy a plain business suit, one that she could wear again and again. Lucas had nixed that idea, if she believed Abby.

Abby unpinned the veil, careful not to disturb Susannah's hair. She'd felt a little silly curling it to fall around her face, as if she were a teenager trying to impress the boys. But Abby had insisted it looked more bridal than her normal bun.

"You look beautiful," Abby whispered and kissed her on her cheek.

"Are you ready for some cake?" Lucas asked, stepping in front of her a few minutes later. "You took off your veil?"

"Yes, it was giving me a headache," she replied.

"You look beautiful," he repeated Abby's words

without the kiss. It bothered Susannah that his words meant more to her than Abby's. The husky catch in his voice sent an unwanted shiver down her spine.

Taking her hand, he helped her to her feet and escorted her to the formal dining room where she'd dined last week. The chairs were all pulled back from the lace-covered table, and in its center was a magnificent wedding cake.

"Where…?"

"Frankie made it," Lucas whispered.

The man was standing by the door to the kitchen and Susannah left Lucas's side to kiss Frankie's cheek. "Thank you so much, Frankie. The cake is absolutely gorgeous. I'm so amazed."

He beamed at her. "My pleasure."

"All right, stop flirting with Frankie and come back over here," Lucas called, amid much laughter. As if he were really a jealous groom.

She moved back to the table and he slipped his arm around her waist, pulling her close, then handed her the knife and covered her hand with his. The flash of a camera startled her and she almost dropped the knife.

"Hey! I don't want to lose any toes," Lucas joked. Again, everyone gathered around the cake laughed.

She gulped, not bothering to smile.

He guided the knife to the middle tier of the cake, sliding the knife through the creamy icing and cake beneath. Abby held out a plate for the first piece. Once they'd put down the knife, Lucas took the plate and turned to Susannah. "Ready?"

"You're not going to—" she began, fearing he

meant to smear her face with cake as she'd seen some bridegrooms do. She'd always thought it was childish and cruel, but she'd forgotten to discuss this with Lucas. Because she hadn't realized they'd have such a big reception, or a wedding cake.

He stopped her question by taking a small bite of cake and feeding it daintily into her open mouth. "Chew," he ordered. As she automatically followed his order, he bent over and surprised her with a kiss.

"Hey, Luke, we're never gonna get cake if you don't stop kissing your woman!" some male called out.

Susannah, again lost to his touch, jerked back. She stared at Luke, unsure what to do next. He lifted the plate of cake he was holding just a little higher, catching her attention.

"Oh. It's your turn." She took a larger piece between her fingers, and he opened wide. But as he took the cake into his mouth, he captured her hand. Staring at her, he drew each of her fingers into his mouth, licking the icing from them, one at a time.

"Damn, someone get a water hose. They're going to set the house on fire."

The laughter was even louder, increased by a few cheers, and Susannah thought she'd never been so embarrassed in her life.

"All right, you two. Move aside so we can serve this hungry bunch some cake," Abby ordered, as if nothing unusual had occurred.

And maybe it hadn't. If this had been a usual marriage. But Susannah knew it wasn't. Lucas had as-

122 THE NINE-MONTH BRIDE

sured her it wasn't. So why was he acting as if he'd been in love with her forever?

He pulled her aside and answered her unspoken question at once. "I think we fooled 'em," he whispered in her ear, his arm around her waist. At his touch she felt a familiar current of longing travel through her.

Of course, she should've known. Lucas Boyd would be too proud to let people know his marriage was one of convenience. Probably, in the barn, he'd been telling everyone how crazy she was about him.

The sad thing was, it might be the truth. It would help explain her reaction to him. But he didn't know. Or want to know. And, if she were smart, she'd make sure it wasn't true.

After the cake was served, people began leaving. The crowd thinned out enough that Susannah noticed the huge pile of presents they'd brought. She'd already had a shower Thursday night, receiving some lovely, thoughtful gifts. It had surprised her that many of them were personal. She now owned an array of beautiful nightgowns and underwear.

One of which she would wear tonight.

Quickly she shifted her thoughts. She'd never make it through to the end of the reception if she started thinking about what was to come.

Lucas couldn't focus on the conversations going on around him. All he could think about was tonight.

When the reception was over, he and Susannah would go upstairs and consummate their marriage. And make a child.

"There he goes again," one of his cowboys said, punching his friend with his elbow. "He drifts off, with that look on his face. Think maybe he's worried about the herd?" Then he laughed uproariously as if he'd made a witty comment.

"What are you talking about?" Lucas asked.

"Don't mind Mike. He thinks you're thinking about what's going to happen after we leave," one of his neighbors explained.

"Yeah," Mike chimed in, "and we ain't talking about the cleaning up!" He laughed again.

Several others joined him as Lucas felt his cheeks redden. Hell, he hadn't realized he'd been so open.

Another neighbor, older, made a big production of looking at his watch. "It is getting late. Probably we should all pack it in."

"Late? Hell, it's only eight o'clock," Mike protested. "I think we should make another run at the food. You've still got enough to feed an army."

Lucas considered telling him to have all the food he wanted—to go. He didn't want to be inhospitable, but he was ready for the reception to end. He looked over the guests' heads, searching for Susannah.

Fortunately for his patience, some of his neighbors decided an early departure was called for and began a general movement toward the door. Which meant, of course, that Susannah would come to tell them bye.

So he didn't have to search for her anymore.

Instead they reversed the procedure for the afternoon, staying by the door to tell their well-wishers goodbye.

By the time the last of them, Doc and Abby, had left, it was closer to ten than nine. He thought Susannah looked even more tense than she had earlier.

"Why don't you go on up and get ready. I'll help Frankie straighten the furniture for a few minutes." He thought it was a tactful way to give her some time alone.

She didn't even smile. With a stiff nod, she hurried up the stairs, as if escaping.

He stared after her, frowning. What was wrong? Everything had gone well. They'd convinced the entire town that they were in love. That they were eager for their wedding bed.

Well, maybe that last thought hadn't taken much work. There was some kind of chemical reaction every time he touched her. It wasn't love. He was sure of that, but his body responded to that lady like a stick of dynamite to a match.

"Hey, boss, I don't need no help. Most of it can be left until tomorrow," Frankie assured him.

"It's okay. The groom is supposed to give the bride a little time to herself."

"Oh. It's a good thing I never married. I woulda messed up good, 'cause I wouldn't be able to wait. She's some looker, Mrs. Boyd. And nice, too."

"Yeah. I didn't think she was pretty at first, but she kind of grows on you."

They moved the chairs back around the table in the dining room. When they finished there, Frankie started into the living room, assuming Lucas would follow.

He stopped and stared up the stairs.

"Uh, Frankie, I think I'll go on up, now, if you don't mind."

"Right. I'll go to the bunkhouse for tonight, but I'll cook breakfast for you in the morning."

"Uh, okay, but probably not till eight."

He figured his wife could sleep in the day after her wedding. Hell, Beth had slept in most of the time, especially when she was pregnant. She said she wasn't a morning person.

Suddenly realizing he didn't know if Susannah was a morning person or not, he hurried up the stairs. Not that it mattered, but...he felt funny, knowing so little about his bride.

Except that he wanted her more than he'd ever wanted a woman in his life.

But it was only because of that strange chemistry.

Unexplainable but true.

He took the last two steps in one and reached the door to his bedroom. Mindful of her possible shyness, he rapped before he opened it.

With a smile on his face, he stepped in and came to an abrupt halt. There was no sign of Susannah here. No suitcases. No bed turned down. No scent of perfume in the air.

He crossed the room to the bathroom door. Another knock before he impatiently opened it. Nothing. No feminine clothes, no makeup, or the usual clutter a woman left in the bathroom. He hadn't realized, until that minute, how much he'd missed that feminine presence.

Where was she?

The thought that she had changed her mind and

returned to town was enough to take his breath away. He charged through the bedroom, throwing open his door, preparing to shout at Frankie, when the door across from his opened.

Chapter Nine

She stood there, pale and trembling, in a simple silk gown in shell pink that brought out red highlights in her long hair. Her teeth sank into her bottom lip and troubled eyes met his.

He looked over her shoulder. There were her bags. The wedding dress was laid across the bed. White pumps were beside it. "Frankie must've put your things in the wrong room. Our bedroom is across the hall."

"No. I didn't think you'd want to share a room, since—" She broke off and stared at her feet. When he said nothing, she added, "So I took this one, if you don't mind."

He stared at her blankly. What could he say? *No, I want you in my bed every night.* That made him sound like a demanding, insensitive male. "Okay."

When she didn't move, he slowly reached out and took her hand. She didn't resist, so he tugged her toward him. "But we'll, uh, you'll come to my bed. My son is going to be conceived in my bed, okay?"

To his relief, she didn't refuse.

But she also didn't exhibit any enthusiasm for what lay ahead. He didn't understand why. He might be distracted by his reaction to her every time he touched her, but he knew she responded, too. In fact, it was that response that put him over the top.

He'd loved Beth with all his heart. But the physical side of marriage hadn't interested her. She "did her duty" but found pleasure in other things.

Unaware of his thoughts, Susannah stepped into his room. Her gaze focused on the king-size bed, and she stopped. He frowned, unsure what to do next. Was she afraid of making love?

He touched her arm and found it icy cold. As if— if she were a virgin. That thought slammed into him with all the strength of an earthquake.

"Susannah, you're not—I mean, you have—damn it, this isn't your first time, is it?"

Her cheeks flooded with color and she barely nodded.

"You are?" He hadn't believed any woman over the age of twenty was inexperienced.

"I'm sorry."

Her soft apology awakened him from his surprise and brought a frown to his face. "You have nothing to apologize for, Susannah. I wasn't aware— It makes no difference."

She swallowed convulsively. "I—I don't know how—" She broke off and looked away.

All her concern, her nervousness was suddenly explained, and Lucas breathed a sigh of relief. With a smile, he added, ''That's okay. I do know how. Everything will be fine, Susannah.''

She nodded but said nothing, still not looking at him.

''I like your nightgown,'' he said softly, running a finger up her bare arm to slip beneath the strap. She shivered and shot him a quick glance before dropping her gaze again.

He moved closer.

''Is it new?'' he asked, both hands now caressing her arms.

It had been a long time since he'd seduced a woman. An inexperienced woman. He hadn't run across one of those very often. Usually he'd moved on.

But he found the need to seduce Susannah incredibly attractive. And he couldn't quite extinguish a feeling of satisfaction that he would be her first. And her last. Bending over, he kissed her on the corner of her sexy lips. ''You smell good, too.''

''So—so do you.''

''I haven't had my shower yet. You won't go away if I take a quick one, will you?''

It bothered him that she seemed to welcome the respite his shower offered. Her shy smile almost had him changing his mind. But it was her wedding night. He wanted everything perfect.

''Just make yourself at home. I won't be a minute.'' He backed to the bathroom door, relief flooding him as she walked to the bed and sat down on its edge.

* * *

She'd almost melted.

When he'd touched her, she'd had to fight to keep from throwing her arms around his neck, pressing her body against his, begging for his kiss.

Thank goodness she'd been able to control herself, to keep him from knowing how needy she was. They were going to make a baby, not love. And he would be embarrassed to know that she wanted his touch, craved his caress. She still couldn't quite believe her reaction to him.

She closed her eyes and concentrated on control. On pretending to be blasé about what was about to happen. On pretending.

True to his word, Lucas opened the bathroom door in no time. She gulped as he stood before her, a towel wrapped around his waist.

His broad, hairy chest tapered to slim hips and muscular legs and she couldn't stop staring. She'd been an only child and her limited experience with her fiancé, much to his disappointment, hadn't involved disrobing.

"Am I embarrassing you?" he asked, moving toward her, a grin on his face. "I could get dressed, but then I'd have to take it all off again. It didn't seem worth the effort."

His relaxed air was a novelty, one that eased Susannah's tension. She didn't know lovers could find amusement as well as possible passion. With a hesitant smile, she said, "I'd hate for you to waste all that energy."

"My thoughts exactly. I'd much rather put it to better use."

She shivered, her eyes growing wide.

"You look like Little Red Riding Hood when the Big Bad Wolf said he wanted to eat her. Do I scare you?"

No, I scare myself. "No, of course not."

"Good." He reached the bed. "Want me to turn back the covers?"

"Oh! I can—can do that." She stood, glad for something to do, and pulled back the bedspread and sheet. As she straightened, strong arms slid around her waist and his lips lightly caressed her shoulder.

She held herself still, not sure what her reaction should be. When he did nothing else, she looked over her shoulder.

"Look, Susannah, let's make a pact."

Turning to face him, she waited for him to explain. Had he changed his mind? Was he going to suggest they turn to Doc, as she had suggested earlier?

"This is an awkward situation. So I think we should be honest with each other. If I do something you don't like, that makes you uncomfortable, just tell me."

"And you'll tell me if I do something wrong?" she asked, relief filling her.

He pulled her close against him and she was startled to feel his arousal through the towel. "I think that's highly unlikely. I haven't been with a woman in a long time, sweetheart, and I'm liable to embarrass myself at any moment."

It hadn't occurred to her that he might be nervous

or concerned about his performance. Immediately she yearned to set him at ease. Her lips planted butterfly kisses on his face, as she'd dreamed of doing.

As if she'd detonated a bomb, their lovemaking exploded. His mouth devoured hers even as his hands urged the gown up her body. Her hands roamed his chest, delighting in the hard muscles.

Before she knew it, her gown and panties and his towel had fallen to the floor and the two of them were stretched out on the bed. He covered her body with his as he intimately stroked and caressed her skin, and she met him at every turn.

When he entered her, his lips returned to hers, urging her to join in the frantic pleasure, but she needed no encouragement. She'd never experienced such joy, such oneness, even though there was a temporary discomfort. She hadn't even known making love could be so pleasurable.

Everything seemed to explode at once, and Susannah wasn't sure if she lost consciousness or not. When she opened her eyes, filled with incredulous joy, Lucas's eyes remained closed. His body slid from hers, and he slumped beside her. His mouth moved, mumbling something, but she couldn't understand the words.

And he slept.

She lay beside him, her gaze tracing the strength of his body. It occurred to her that, had she been asked, she would never have agreed to make love with the light on. But she hadn't even remembered to be self-conscious once Lucas touched her.

Had he realized? Had it been obvious that she'd been overwhelmed by his lovemaking?

Strangely enough, her thoughts turned to Beth, his wife. Poor Beth. She had had Lucas as her husband, had shared his bed, had conceived his child, had owned his heart.

Now Susannah would have all but the last, if she was lucky. Her emotions changed from remorse for Beth to sadness for herself. Because owning Lucas's heart suddenly seemed a prize beyond belief.

Enough, Susannah. No feeling sorry for yourself. You've made your bed, so lie in it. She almost giggled. Not many women would complain about the bed she'd made, as long as Lucas Boyd filled it.

And he'd given her an incredible gift. She wasn't frigid. In fact, she had to fight herself now to keep a distance between their two bodies.

So she had nothing to complain about.

To ensure that she maintained control, she'd have to go back to her bedroom. Otherwise, she wouldn't be able to keep her hands off him. Even now, she wanted to stroke him all over, to learn his body, every indentation, every muscle. To meet his lips with hers.

And he wanted to sleep.

With one last, long, greedy look, she slid from the bed. Picking up her nightgown and bikini panties, she returned to her sanctuary.

And dreamed of Lucas.

Lucas opened one eye, a smile on his face. Why was he feeling so wonderful? Then he remembered.

Susannah. And the incredible lovemaking they'd shared.

He reached out for her warm body. And found nothing. Both eyes popped open and he sat up. The lights were still on. He had no difficulty seeing that he was alone.

He sprang from the bed and hurried to the closed door. Crossing the hall, he eased open the door to the room across from his. It was dark, but he could see the faint outline of her body under the covers. She was alseep.

Frowning, he closed the door. He didn't want her in that room. He wanted her in his bed. Had he upset her? Done something wrong? Disgusted her with his uncontrollable passion?

The last few moments with her in his arms had gone by incredibly fast. He hadn't spent much time holding her before he'd taken his pleasure.

Damn! He hadn't meant to be so selfish. But it had been so long for him, his body had taken control. He thought Susannah had received some pleasure, because he remembered a sweet moan that had urged him on. And her lips touching him as he'd kissed her incredible body.

He opened the door again, his gaze tracing her outline. He wanted to scoop her up in his arms, carry her back to his bed and tell her she could never leave. He even took a step toward her.

His conscience stopped him. They'd agreed to make a child. He'd warned her there would be no emotion. She'd chosen a bedroom separate from him.

She wanted her privacy.

He wanted her.

He closed the door again. Okay, so he'd give her privacy. For a while. They'd ease into this marriage business slowly. Maybe they could become friends.

As long as they continued to be lovers. For whatever reason, Susannah gave him more pleasure than he'd ever experienced. A pleasure that he longed to repeat as soon as possible.

But she didn't want to wake up beside him. She didn't want more lovemaking tonight. She didn't want him to touch her, to hold her against him.

Even thinking about such actions caused a reaction in him. He backed across the hall into his room and shut the door. It was the only way to ensure that he didn't spoil everything.

And the next time he made love to Susannah, he would take it slower, give her pleasure before he took his own.

He couldn't wait.

After a shower the next morning, Susannah dressed in slacks and a shirt and made the courageous trek to the kitchen. She wasn't sure how she would be able to face Lucas this morning.

She didn't have long to wait. He was leaning against the kitchen counter, talking to Frankie as he rinsed some dishes.

As soon as Lucas saw her, he crossed the room to greet her. With a brief kiss, before nodding in Frankie's direction. "Frankie thought maybe you'd like some cinnamon rolls for breakfast this morning."

She understood his meaning. Thankfully her lips

hadn't clung to his, as they'd wanted to. He was kissing her for Frankie's benefit. She cleared her throat.

"That's very thoughtful of you, Frankie, but really, it isn't necessary to go to so much trouble."

"No trouble. How about some coffee, too?"

"I'd love some."

To her surprise, it was Lucas who brought her coffee as she sat down at the table. "You shouldn't wait on me, Lucas. I could've—"

"Hey, it's your first day in your new home. I think that deserves a little pampering," he said and sat down beside her.

Frankie brought a plate of warm cinnamon rolls to the table and then added a bowl of fresh fruit from the refrigerator.

Nervous, Susannah smiled at the man. "Won't you join us for a coffee break, Frankie? You must've been up early to make these rolls."

A smile broke across his face. "I don't mind if I do. Boss, you want more coffee before I sit down?"

Lucas shoved his cup forward as an answer. After pouring more coffee, Frankie joined them. Susannah struggled to eat, under two pairs of eagle eyes, while the men didn't hesitate to finish several rolls.

"When you're through, we probably need to start opening gifts," Lucas told her. "We got a delivery this morning from the church. Seems a lot of people left presents there, as well. You're going to be writing thank-you notes for months."

Susannah turned to look at him. "What's this *you*, Tonto? I thought we were in this together."

It was Lucas's turn to stare. "What do you mean?"

"I mean *we* will be writing thank-you notes. Not just me." She smiled at his reaction.

"But that's woman's work," he protested, rearing back in his chair.

"Come into the nineties," she suggested dryly.

"Susannah, I mean Mrs. Boyd, is right, Lucas. Men are supposed to do lady things these days. It says so in the magazines," Frankie assured him.

"When did you read a ladies' magazine?" Lucas demanded, glaring at his cook.

"At the dentist's office in the Springs last year. You wouldn't believe what they put in those magazines."

"Thank you for your support, Frankie. And, please, call me Susannah. It will take me a while to remember to respond to Mrs. Boyd." She blinked several times as Lucas turned his glare on her. Was he upset that she expected him to help with the thank-you notes?

"All right. I'll do it, but you've got to help, too, Frankie," he suddenly said.

"Me? I can't write no thank-you notes."

"No, but you can help open the presents. You and I will do the grunt work and Susannah can make a list of who gave us what."

Susannah downed her last sip of coffee and rose. "That sounds like a good plan. Let me rinse these dishes and—"

"Here now, Susannah, that's my job," Frankie

protested. "You're not thinking of doing me out of my job, are you?"

"Of course not, Frankie. I couldn't do it half so well as you. But I don't need to be waited on."

Frankie seemed pleased with her response, even as Lucas stared at her, frowning. She didn't know what she'd done to upset him this morning, but she was pleased that Frankie would be with them. It eased the awkwardness a little.

She'd thought the matter of opening presents would be quickly resolved, but when she entered the living room, the pile she'd seen last night seemed to have multiplied like rabbits.

"Good heavens! I didn't expect—this is too much."

"Yeah," Lucas agreed, rubbing his nape in embarrassment. "Seems folks were real happy about me marryin' again."

She watched him, her gaze greedily following every movement. She wasn't surprised. For this man to be a hermit would be an incredible waste.

"Here's paper and a pen," Frankie said, entering the room.

"Well, let's get started," Lucas ordered.

They worked for several hours, sharing laughter and appreciation for the various gifts they received. A handmade quilt almost brought tears to Susannah's eyes, and she stroked the soft material as it lay across her lap.

Lucas followed the movement of those hands, remembering how they'd touched him last night. And hungered for them to do so again.

His instincts had been right. Susannah would be a wonderful mother. Her gentle hands would console and love a child.

The bootjack, in the shape of a big frog, brought a different reaction. Amid giggles that felt like champagne bubbles in his stomach, she stared at the metal creation.

"Show me how it works," she insisted, pulling on Lucas's arm.

"Haven't you used one before?"

"No. I don't own any boots."

He eyed her slender feet. "We'll correct that situation real soon."

"Why would I need them?"

"Darlin'," he drawled, "you're living on a ranch now. You're the rancher's wife. Of course you'll need boots."

She stared at him but offered no argument. He put one foot on the jack and the heel of his other boot in the notch and pulled. The boot slid off.

"Oh, I like that," she said, clapping her hands.

He raised one eyebrow, but a smile tugged at his lips. She liked a lot of things. He hoped one of them was his lovemaking.

After lunch, organized by Frankie with the leftover food from the night before, Lucas put an end to their work. "We'll finish later. I need a break."

"But we could—"

"Nope," he returned to Susannah's protest. "You could use a nap. Yesterday was pretty stressful."

"A nap? I never—"

"I'll go check on the bunkhouse," Frankie said and left the room. At least one person had understood his intention. Unfortunately, it wasn't the one he was interested in.

"Did we offend Frankie?" Susannah asked, looking at him curiously.

"Nope. He was just getting out of the way."

"Out of the way of what?"

"Our going upstairs to my bed."

He'd shocked her. That much was clear.

"But—but it's the middle of the day." Her lower lip was trembling again.

"I know, but it takes real dedication to make a baby. Night and day." When she looked doubtful, he desperately asked, "Want to call Doc to ask him? I'm sure I'm right about this."

"Of course not!" she exclaimed, her cheeks reddening. "I just—I didn't—"

"Hell, sweetheart, if it makes you uncomfortable we can confine our efforts to darkness, but it may take us a little longer." It hurt that she wasn't as eager as he was, but that wasn't going to stop him. He was too hungry for her. Unless she said no.

"No, of course I'm willing—I didn't know—I mean—" She broke off, as if she couldn't figure out what to say.

He took her hand and pulled her to her feet, sending the duly recorded list to the floor. Then he scooped her up into his arms and headed for the stairs.

"Lucas, I'm too heavy. You'll hurt yourself."

"I'm gonna hurt myself if I don't get you in my bed, lady," he assured her as he climbed the stairs. By the time he reached the top, his breathing was heavy. But he wasn't sure if the exertion caused it, or if her body pressed against his chest was the reason.

After pushing past the door and shutting it behind him, he looked into Susannah's eyes. To his relief, she smiled at him.

"I wouldn't want you to be injured," she assured him softly and held her lips up for his kiss.

Chapter Ten

Susannah prepared for work the next morning, her cautious heart wondering if she could really be happy living with the man she had developed a craving for...but didn't love, she hurriedly assured herself.

She'd learned a lot yesterday. That sex was as good in sunlight as moonlight with Lucas Boyd. That pillow talk provided an intimacy she'd never experienced, one that brought smiles to the bedroom, another new experience. Even though Lucas's gentle teasing held nothing significant and didn't mean he cared about her, it represented a closeness new to her.

And she learned that she was no more frigid than the hottest salsa served south of the border. She didn't know why, except perhaps that incredible chemistry between them. Or maybe he was a superlative lover. But he could melt her bones with a look. When he touched her, she had no resistance at all.

So, all in all, she descended the stairs that Monday morning with a good feeling about the future. When she entered the kitchen, she headed straight for the coffeepot, needing caffeine to substitute for the lack of sleep their lovemaking had caused.

"Morning," Frankie called.

"Good morning. I could get used to you having a pot of coffee ready every morning, Frankie. I'm being spoiled."

"You got to have more than coffee. Sit down and I'll fix you breakfast."

"Just a piece of toast, please. I'm running late."

"Where are you going?"

It wasn't Frankie who asked that question, but her husband, Lucas, standing just inside the back door.

She raised her eyebrows. "To work, of course."

"Nonsense. You're my wife. You don't need to work," he asserted firmly as he stepped forward to the coffeepot.

Shaking her head to clear it, she waited until he had his first sip of coffee before she answered. She kept her response mild, not wanting to argue. "Really?"

He must've thought that word indicated amazement at his generosity. With a smile, he leaned forward to brush her lips with his. "Of course, sweetheart. I told you I'd provide—" He halted to glance at Frankie. "We're okay financially."

Anger rose in her. He thought he could simply dictate her life? Without saying anything to him, she turned to Frankie. "I'll be back a little after five,

Frankie. If you have something to do, I can fix dinner.''

Then she turned to leave, only to be stopped by Lucas's hand on her arm. "Didn't you hear me?"

"Of course I did," she responded, struggling to hold on to her control.

"Then why are you going to work?"

"Because I want to. Because I committed myself to the job before I ever met you. Because a librarian is who I am. Because you're going to work today, so why shouldn't I?" She finished by drawing the breath she'd suspended during her rapid-fire response.

"Because you don't have to," he countered, his voice more forceful.

With a coldness she wouldn't have believed possible when she'd shared his bed the night before, she only said, "Excuse me."

Her effort to move past him failed.

"Damn it! Why won't you listen to me? We had an agree—" Again he halted and looked at Frankie. "Uh, we'd better go to my office to discuss this."

"I don't have time. I'm going to be late as it is." She tugged at his hold on her but was unable to break loose.

Lucas appeared stunned that she didn't fall in with his suggestion at once. "You are my wife!" he roared. "You'll do as I say!"

It was just as well she hadn't gone into the marriage with rose-colored glasses on, she thought. The honeymoon was definitely over. "I will do as I think best, Lucas Boyd, and nothing you can do will change that. Now, turn loose of my arm.''

"You promised to obey me Saturday!" he reminded her.

"No, I didn't. The pastor asked me if I objected to that wording just before the ceremony. He left it out. You should've listened." She gave a powerful jerk on her arm and escaped out the door. Wasting no time, she hurried to her car and drove off.

Lucas stood there fuming.

He could've caught up with her, of course, but what would he have done with her then? He had no idea. After yesterday, he'd thought the marriage idea had been a brilliant move. Now he wasn't so sure.

"Boss, you can't talk to her like that. That women's magazine said—''

"Frankie, I will not allow your afternoon in the dentist's office to rule my marriage."

"I don't know why not. It lasted almost as long," Frankie muttered as he sidled out the back door, escaping his boss's temper.

When Lucas finally returned to the barn after ranting in solitude about the contrariness of a certain woman, he discovered that his difficulties were well-known. His men, apparently thrilled with the changes in him since Susannah came into his life, offered several hints to help him get along with his bride.

"You gotta sweet-talk women."

"Flowers are a good thing."

"It don't hurt none to have a working wife."

"You oughtta apologize."

He finally exploded. "Mind your own business! I'll take care of Susannah. She's *my* wife."

The cowboys slinked away to their various jobs, leaving him alone again, feeling lower to the ground than a pig's belly.

And the only thing that would make him feel better was for a certain contrary woman to return home that evening.

In spite of their disagreement about her work, something they never discussed again, Susannah found a satisfying routine in her new life. She spent her day doing the work she loved. Then she returned home to her husband. That word never ceased to thrill her.

Each night, after she went upstairs, he would knock on her door and lead her to his bed. There was no discussion, only a desire that enflamed them when they touched.

After their lovemaking, Susannah, in spite of Lucas's requests for her to stay, returned to her own bed. It was her only protection from complete submission to his powerful presence. But she longed to wrap herself in his strong arms, to snuggle against him, listening to the rise and fall of his breath. Feeling his hands as they roamed her body, feather touches that sent shimmers across her skin.

But she denied herself those pleasures.

She dreaded the arrival of the wrong time of the month for their lovemaking. She was becoming addicted to his touch. In a normal marriage, the husband and wife might still cuddle, whisper in the dark, hold each other as they fell asleep. But Lucas had no interest in those things.

So she waited with dread.

Only her period never came.

When she was a week late, she drove on Saturday all the way into Colorado Springs to an anonymous drugstore to purchase several pregnancy kits.

Lucas protested the trip without knowing the reason for it. He'd made plans to show her around the ranch. While she would have loved the attention, she felt an urgency to discover if she was pregnant.

She waited another week. Then, the next Saturday morning, she took the test. It was positive.

Now she faced a true dilemma. If she told Lucas she was pregnant, he would be thrilled. But he also wouldn't see a need for them to continue to make love.

While Susannah was thrilled, also, at the idea of a child, her child, she mourned the loss of intimacy with Lucas. Her mood that day, as he gave her the postponed tour of his beloved land, alternated between despondency and exhilaration.

"Are you all right?" Lucas asked her after a couple of hours.

"Yes, of course!" she gasped. "What do you mean?"

"You seemed distracted," he said pointedly, reaching over to cover her clasped hands. "Are you sure you're not wearing yourself out with the job?"

It was the first time he'd mentioned her job since their argument. "No. I enjoy my work."

With a grunt he accelerated, leaving the south pasture behind. "Want to see my prized Black Angus bull? We call him Rocky, but that's not his registered name." He rattled off a scientific-sounding name.

"Is he big?"

"He's huge. But he's as tame as a baby." His gaze drifted to her stomach and she sat up straighter. Had he guessed her secret?

It was the first time they'd spent so much time in each other's company since the Sunday after their wedding. Susannah found herself charmed all over again with Lucas's gentlemanly behavior, his teasing. He might not love her, but he was kind.

They shared a picnic lunch that Frankie had prepared. Lucas urged her to eat more when she picked at her food. But she was discovering a queasy stomach with her pregnancy.

Before Lucas could wonder at how little she ate, he was distracted by the weather. It was November now, and the clouds had built up suddenly.

"We'd better pack it in and get back to the house."

"Why?" Had she displeased him?

"I think we're going to have our first real snowstorm of the winter. We don't want to get trapped out here."

He'd been right. The snow closed in on them as they pulled in near the barn. He sent her into the house. That night, when he came in, Frankie had built a fire in the fireplace for them, and she snuggled in his arms before a dying fire, contentment filling her.

"You don't mind the snow?" he asked, his arm wrapped around her.

"No, I like cold weather." The man would have to be blind to think she was unhappy, she decided with a smile. In fact, she'd never been happier.

When he led her upstairs to his bed, she was glad she hadn't shared her news with him. She wanted more days like today, more possibilities to share their inner selves with each other. Somewhere, in the back of her mind, hovered the idea that their marriage might become a true one, filled with exchanges and togetherness.

December. Lucas emerged from his room at his normal time, even though he wouldn't start work quite as early. The days were growing shorter and the chores lighter with the wintertime.

But hell, why not get up at his regular time? He had no reason to linger under the warm covers. His wife refused to share his bed. Oh, she'd let him make love to her. In fact, she'd met him more than half-way. Her innocent joy in his touch, the sweet moans that slipped out as he loved her, her utter contentment afterward, made his control problematic.

He'd blamed his need for her on the three years he'd remained celibate, but after six weeks of love-making almost every day, he had to admit he wanted her. More and more.

He paused as he passed Susannah's door. Some noise had distracted him. Leaning closer, he thought it sounded like someone throwing up.

Was Susannah sick? He almost bolted through the

closed door before a thought struck him. *She might be pregnant.* Some women experienced morning sickness, he knew, though Beth never had.

Exhilaration filled him. His son. The child he needed. The reason he'd entered a loveless marriage. The reason he and Susannah—his joy came to a screeching halt. If Susannah was pregnant, there would be no need for those nights in his bed. She might refuse to ever let him touch her again.

He turned to stone, his mind frantically dealing with those revelations. He didn't want to give up the intimacy he'd found with Susannah.

What was the hurry? If she didn't tell him she was pregnant, he didn't have to admit it. He could continue making love to her. Maybe she didn't know, yet. She probably thought she had the flu.

Or maybe she did have the flu. He was no doctor. Only her lover.

He tiptoed down the stairs, pretending he never heard her physical distress. She'd have to tell him before he'd give up those incredible nights with her in his bed.

Christmas Day. Last Christmas Susannah had been in the throes of decision-making. She'd been living in Denver, alone, after her mother's death, trying to decide what to do with herself.

Alone. Unhappy.

Then, she'd taken the job in Caliente. And decided to have a child.

She rubbed her still flat stomach. She'd noticed a slight thickening of her waist, a sensitivity to her breasts, that confirmed the pregnancy test. She was going to have to see Dr. Grable soon.

But not before she told her husband.

She'd decided today was the day. His gift, along with a fine leather wallet and some new cologne, would be his child. Today, beside the Christmas tree she'd decorated with her family's special ornaments, she would tell Lucas that his wish had come true.

Abby and Dr. Grable were joining them for Christmas dinner. Susannah spent the morning in the kitchen helping Frankie prepare the meal.

"Susannah, I can't thank you enough for that Cuisinart. I've been wantin' one of those things for a long time," Frankie told her as he operated the new machine.

"But why didn't you tell Lucas? He would've bought you one." She knew Lucas appreciated Frankie's work and wouldn't have hesitated to provide him with anything he requested.

"Aw, I didn't *need* it. The boss was feelin' so bad, it seemed low-down to bother him."

Susannah was touched by Frankie's concern. She kissed him on the cheek. "You're a good man, Frankie."

"Hey, what's this? You trying to seduce my wife, Frankie?" Lucas called from the doorway. He laughed when Frankie turned red in the face and jumped away from Susannah.

"Shame on you, Lucas Boyd," she reprimanded. "I was expressing our appreciation to Frankie."

He crossed to her side and casually slid an arm around her shoulders. More and more, he touched her freely, making her feel he was more comfortable with her as each day went by.

"Sorry, Frankie. But I figured that expensive machine told him we appreciated him. I hate to see the bills come in after Christmas. You bought every cowboy on the ranch a present. They're all calling you Santa Claus."

He was grinning at her, so she didn't think he really minded her gifts. Besides, there would be no bills. She'd paid for everything herself.

"They work hard" was Susannah's only comment.

"So do I. Is there something for me under the tree?"

"Aw, boss, you know there is. I caught you looking at the tags on the boxes the other day," Frankie said.

"Quit giving away my secrets," Lucas protested. Then he pulled Susannah under the mistletoe hanging over the door and kissed her.

Maybe she was going to get her wish for Christmas, too. She wanted a real marriage, a real husband, because she was discovering she couldn't do without Lucas Boyd. And she was afraid that feeling was called love.

Dinner had been served and greatly appreciated. The dishes had been cleared and Frankie had gone to join the other men at the bunkhouse. Then presents were opened. Susannah had taken special care in gifts for Abby and Doc.

After all, they'd had a part in the changes in her life.

As she rose to gather the wrapping paper and throw it away, Doc got up to help.

In the kitchen, he asked softly, "You feeling okay?"

Susannah jumped in surprise. "What do you mean?"

"You've changed a little. I just wondered—"

"I'll be in for an appointment next week," she admitted, unwilling to say the actual words before she told Lucas.

"Ah. Good." He said nothing else, and Susannah knew he wouldn't reveal anything to Lucas. But she was on needles and pins the rest of the evening. Lucas had to be the first to know.

After Abby and Doc had left, Lucas drew her down on the couch in front of the glowing Christmas tree. With his arm around her, her body pressed to his, he smiled at her.

"I want you to know I appreciate your efforts for Christmas. The whole place is happier. Those idiotic cowboys tell me every day how lucky I am to have you around here. Every last one of them would do anything you asked."

"They're sweet."

"Come on, Susannah, they're men. No one ever called them sweet before." He pulled her a little closer.

"I'm glad everyone was pleased. Did you like your presents?"

"Of course. I've been needing a new wallet and the—"

"I haven't given you your real present." She held her breath, excited but afraid.

"You haven't? But I don't have anything else to give you," he said with a frown.

She fingered the diamond ear studs he'd given her. She'd never owned such expensive jewelry. "You gave me more than enough. My earrings are beautiful."

"So what's my other present?"

She hesitated and then whispered, "Your child."

Unsure what his reaction would be, she waited as he grew absolutely still, not moving. Wasn't he happy?

He removed his arm from her shoulders and slewed around to almost face her. "You're sure?"

She nodded.

"When?"

"I think around the first of August. I'll go see Doc next week."

"He knows?"

"I haven't told him. He asked about my health today, so I think he suspects."

"Are you feeling all right?"

He looked worried, a frown on his brow. Susannah couldn't resist smoothing it away with her fingers. "I'm fine. I get a little sick in the mornings, but that's all."

"You should stop work at once," he ordered.

"No."

"Susannah, be sensible. I don't want you to take any risks. This baby—"

Her heart sank. She'd hoped for an avowal of love. Instead she'd received what she should've expected. Concern for his child.

Unable to bear the disappointment, she rose to her feet. "I'm going to bed now. Thank you for my earrings."

"Susannah—" he called but she ignored him. The tears sliding down her cheeks wouldn't allow her to stay near him. She would hide in her room to lick her wounds. Alone.

No, not alone. She and her child would be together.

Lucas sat on the couch alone. He'd upset her, but he wasn't sure how. He'd suspected for several weeks that she was pregnant, but it had suited him not to know.

Now, he no longer had a choice. He couldn't pretend a need to plant his seed in her. To hold her in his arms, to revel in the sensations she aroused in him every time he touched her.

But in exchange, he had knowledge of his son. His child. His reason for the future. He lost himself in dreams of the child with whom he would build the future. But the picture wasn't as bright as he'd once thought it would be.

Because of Susannah. He didn't know what to do about Susannah. Tonight, he'd climb those stairs, as he had every night since his wedding. But would

Susannah be receptive to his touch? Would she willingly come to his room, melt into his arms?

He paced the floor, debating what he should do until the hour had advanced more than he'd realized. Finally creeping up the stairs, he opened her door without knocking. She lay in her bed, the covers pulled snugly around her, her back to the door.

With a grieving that shocked him, he quietly closed the door and turned to his own room, alone. She had no interest in him anymore. He'd given her what she wanted, a child.

He slid into his bed, prepared to dream of his child. Instead, he found himself mourning his loss of Susannah.

Chapter Eleven

Susannah awoke the next morning at her normal time. But that was the only thing normal. She hadn't visited Lucas's bed last night. He had let her go to her room, and he hadn't disturbed her.

Because he had what he wanted.

Oh, how she'd hoped he would still want her. She should've known. After all, she was inexperienced. While he'd never complained about her lovemaking, she'd feared he might not enjoy it as much as she.

Tears seeped from her eyes, as they'd done last night. She hadn't realized how much she'd counted on their marriage being real. But she had. Because she'd fallen in love with that ornery man.

The father of her child.

She dressed and went downstairs. She couldn't hide in her room all day because her dreams hadn't come true. Even after the baby was born, she still had to face Lucas each day, pretending not to love him. Pretending not to want him. She might as well learn to hide her feelings today.

Besides, the library was closed both today and to-morrow. She wasn't sure what she was going to do with herself, but she'd find something.

Frankie was in the kitchen and greeted her with a cup of coffee and toast.

"Where's Lucas?"

"He went to the barn half an hour ago. Didn't seem in a very good mood. Hope he's not catching the flu that's going around," Frankie said, frowning.

Susannah's heart leaped in spite of her warnings to herself. Maybe he was missing the lovemaking. Maybe he'd bring her back to his bed. Maybe...she'd better think of something besides the bedroom.

When the door opened as she was finishing her coffee, however, she couldn't help searching his face eagerly for some telltale sign that he'd missed her last night.

He ignored her completely, concentrating on the coffeepot rather than her. "It's cold out there."

"Yeah," Frankie agreed. He, too, studied Lucas. "You coming down with something, boss?"

Lucas turned to stare at his cook. "Coming down with what?"

"The flu. Heard it was goin' around."

Lucas shot her a look but she couldn't read his expression. "No, of course not. I'm fine. Slept great last night."

Susannah felt her stomach clench at his words. Drawing a deep breath, she fought to keep her breakfast down. Misery and coffee weren't a good mix for a pregnant woman.

"How about you, Susannah? How did you sleep?" Lucas suddenly asked, staring at her.

Unexpected anger invaded her misery. Was he taunting her? Did he think she would beg for his touch? Did he think he could reject her and she'd still want him? With a control that surprised even her, she smiled at him and said, "Like a baby."

The temperature seemed to drop in the kitchen. Frankie looked up suddenly, his gaze going from one to the other of the pair at the table. "Uh, I gotta put in a load of laundry. Back in a minute."

If she'd hoped for tenderness in their first moment alone, she had to be satisfied with a gruff question. "Are you feeling all right?"

"Fine," she returned.

"No throwing up?"

After successfully battling nausea, she was surprised by her sudden response to his question. She leaped from the chair and just made it to the kitchen sink in time to rid herself of breakfast.

When she felt his hands on her, trying to ease her distress, Susannah couldn't help the shiver that coursed through her. She'd longed for his touch. Straightening, after washing her face, she tried to smile, but she wasn't very successful.

Especially when Lucas immediately dropped his hands and stepped away.

"Have you talked to Doc about throwing up?"

She took a deep breath. "I will when I go to his

office next week, but I understand it's perfectly normal.''

''I think you should call him now. The baby is—''

''I know, Lucas. The baby is all-important.'' Wearily she sank down onto the seat at the table. She already loved this baby with all her heart, but it hurt to be reminded over and over again that, for Lucas, she was nothing more than a means to an end.

After a hesitation, he didn't respond to her words. Instead he asked, ''Do you want anything more to eat?''

Nausea roiled in her stomach again. ''No!'' Out of desperation, she rose and turned toward the door. ''I'm going back to bed.''

Lucas watched the door swing behind her, depression filling him. He hadn't helped her at all. If anything, he'd made her feel worse. What was he going to do?

He thought of his hopes this morning. Somehow, after tossing and turning all night, he'd wondered if Susannah might have missed their lovemaking. If she'd given him any indication that she'd welcome a return to his bed, he'd have carried her upstairs and made glorious love to her. Instead, she'd thrown up.

Did that mean he shouldn't touch her again?

Could he live in the same house with her and not have any contact? He groaned. He'd lived three years without making love to a woman. In mourning for Beth, he couldn't imagine touching another woman.

Then along came Susannah. So different from Beth. But stirring him to even greater heights. He craved her warm body next to his in bed, her arms wrapped around him, her mouth meeting his.

Maybe after the first few months of pregnancy. He'd heard sex was possible almost up until the birth of the baby. He'd talk to Doc. He wouldn't take any chances on the safety of his baby, but he wanted Susannah in his bed.

He strode to the phone and dialed Doc's home number. When Doc's gruff voice answered, he got right down to business. "Doc, should Susannah be throwing up?"

"Is she?"

"Yeah. She lost her breakfast this morning."

"That's fairly normal. Be sure—"

"But Beth didn't."

"Susannah isn't Beth, Lucas," Doc said gently.

"I know that!" he snapped, then apologized.

"I'll give her a thorough checkup next week, boy, but the main thing you need to remember is give her what she wants, be supportive. It's important for the mama-to-be to be happy."

Lucas bowed his head, resting his forehead against the wall. He didn't need to ask his other question. Doc had just answered it for him.

"Thanks, Doc."

"You bet. And congratulations, boy. You did it!"

But it wasn't joy that filled Lucas. When Beth had been pregnant, she'd lost what little interest she'd had in sex. And since Susannah had already indicated she preferred to be left alone, Lucas would have to comply with her wishes.

* * *

Lucas insisted on accompanying Susannah to her first appointment with Doc. Susannah appreciated his concern for his child. She just wished his feelings would extend to her, too.

Since he never touched her now, however, she had to believe it was the baby that caused the continuous frown on his forehead. Her fingers itched to smooth his skin, but she didn't dare touch him. She might break down and plead for him to hold her again.

"Maybe Doc can give you something for your nausea," Lucas suggested.

"I'm doing better since I followed Abby's advice about the crackers by my bed."

"Yeah."

"And I'm sure he'll prescribe vitamins, so the baby will be healthy."

"Doc said to give you whatever you want, to keep you happy, so if there's anything I can do, let me know," he said, keeping his gaze on the road.

Susannah closed her eyes, afraid he'd read the hunger in her gaze. What she wanted was for him to love her. To want her more than life itself. The way she wanted him. But she knew better.

"Okay?" he prodded, still not looking at her.

"Of course. But there's nothing. I'm fine."

He parked the car next to Doc's office and came around to help her out of the pickup, as if she were a precious treasure.

But it wasn't her. It was the baby. At least her child would benefit from his love.

After Doc's examination, with Lucas waiting in his office, the three of them sat down to talk.

"You're perfectly healthy, Susannah, and the baby seems fine. I'm giving you a prescription for vitamins, and I want you to get plenty of rest. These first three months are exhausting."

"Should she quit work?"

Susannah stared at Lucas. She thought they'd settled that question.

"That's up to Susannah, Luke. If she gets too tired, she might. More than likely, though, it would be better if she cut her hours a little. Could you get someone to take over about two or three o'clock, Susannah? That way you could nap before dinner."

She was tempted to assure Doc as well as Lucas that she could work twelve hours a day if she chose. But she buried her obstinacy and said calmly, "Possibly…if I need to. Right now I'm not too tired."

And she'd go crazy sitting in the house longing for Lucas's love.

"Susannah!" Lucas protested.

When he would've said something else, she noticed Doc's frown and shake of his head. Aha, an ally!

They were almost ready to leave, having stood up, when Doc added one more thing. "Oh, and, of course, there's no reason to stop relations. You won't hurt the baby." He smiled as if what he'd just said would make them supremely happy.

With her cheeks flushed, Susannah hurried from the office. Did Doc think their marriage was real? He should know better since he orchestrated it.

Lucas thanked Doc for his words of wisdom and followed his wife from the office. Doc had no idea he'd upset the mother-to-be, but Lucas knew. Susannah couldn't wait to get away from him.

Even helping her from the truck had made her uneasy. He had to remember she'd been a virgin on their wedding night. She wasn't used to a man's needs. And since she was pregnant, her needs took precedence over his hungering for her.

He'd just have to wait until after the baby was born.

Surprisingly, since he'd longed for that moment, the birth of his child, he skipped right over that significant event. All he wanted to know was how long he'd have to wait before he could persuade a nonpregnant Susannah back to his bed.

The first Saturday in March, Susannah slept a little later than usual. After all, she wasn't working today. And Lucas would be out on the ranch working.

She'd taken Doc's advice and cut back on her hours at the library. Each afternoon, she returned to the ranch and crawled into bed for an afternoon nap. Even if she awoke before dinner, she remained in her room until Frankie summoned her for supper.

It was easier that way, because it seemed to her that Lucas was returning to the house earlier and earlier each afternoon. She'd hear his booted step on the stairs, pausing by her door, as if he considered knocking.

She'd hold her breath, wishing he would, knowing he wouldn't. Then he'd continue on into his room.

They'd meet at the dinner table and he'd meticulously ask about her health and that of the baby.

Then they ate in silence. Miserable silence.

Occasionally, when she could bear the silence no longer, she'd come up with some anecdote about her day at the library, but more often than not, she remained silent, too.

Since Christmas Day, when she told him about the baby, it was as if someone had dropped a plastic shield between them. No talking, no touching, no lovemaking.

And she hadn't slept as well. Perhaps it was the naps, but she didn't think so. She'd lain awake in her bed each night, hoping and praying Lucas would seek her out once more.

With a sigh, she dressed and wandered downstairs. Frankie had left the coffeepot ready, but he'd gone to tend to other chores. She'd finally convinced him she could make her own piece of toast.

Downing her glass of milk first before she poured the one cup of coffee Doc allowed her, Susannah rinsed the glass in the sink. Then she got her coffee.

Before she could reach the table, however, she felt something strange. With a gasp, she put her free hand to her stomach.

"What's wrong?" Lucas demanded urgently, from the door.

For the first time since she told him she was pregnant, Susannah smiled naturally at him, excitement erasing all the awkwardness. She couldn't wait to share this moment with him.

"The baby moved. Come quick."

He reached her side and she pressed his big hand to her stomach.

A look of wonderment filled his face as the slight fluttering made itself felt. She looked at him, love and excitement filling her eyes.

Without a word, he scooped her into his arms and headed for the stairs.

He carried her straight to his bed, his lips covering hers before their bodies reached the mattress. The strength of his need was overwhelming. He'd missed her.

When, after an incredible coming together, he began to recover his breath, he wondered why they'd waited so long to be in each other's arms. He could feel the contentment emanating from Susannah as she snuggled against him. There was no murmur of objection as he held her, warm against his heart.

They should have been making love every night, he decided fiercely. What they shared was a gift that not every couple had. Making love. No, he meant having sex— Suddenly he couldn't breathe.

No, he meant making love.

He had done the impossible, the one thing he'd promised himself he wouldn't do. He'd fallen in love with Susannah. No! his heart protested. No, no, no!

Without thinking, he pushed himself away from her, staring at her with horror on his face. He couldn't have made himself vulnerable to such pain again.

Susannah couldn't believe what had just happened. After two months of loneliness, Lucas had renewed her hope, filled her with love, brought her joy about the child together with her love for him.

Smiling, she opened her eyes even as he moved away from her. Before she could stir, she saw the expression on his face. What was wrong?

All her insecurities came rushing back. From the look on his face, he was rejecting her all over again. Not just ignoring her, or avoiding her touch, as he'd done the past two months, but denying any feelings. Regretting what he'd just done.

Regretting the love that filled her.

Sure she had betrayed her feelings, she slid from the bed, grabbing her clothes to press to her body along the way. He hadn't loved her before. He certainly couldn't now that her body had changed, grown larger. She wanted to hide from his gaze.

And she wanted to hide her heart from his rejection.

She ran to her room, slamming the door behind her.

He rapped on the wood almost immediately. "Susannah? Susannah, I'm sorry. I can't—"

No, he couldn't. He couldn't love her as she wanted to be loved. He could only love his child.

With her dreams shattered, her silly, ridiculous dreams of love, she crawled under the covers and wept into her pillow.

He called her name one more time. When she didn't answer, she heard his boots as he walked away.

She couldn't blame him. He'd never promised her he would love her. Only her child.

After telling herself the difficulty was her, not Lucas, the tears finally stopped. But the pain only grew worse. Unable to stop herself, she got up and pulled a suitcase from the closet.

She would accept his behavior. It wasn't his fault, she reminded herself again. *She* was the one who had changed, whose needs were different. How could she have known that Lucas Boyd would melt her frigidity? But she needed some time to shore up her defenses, to hide her wants. Some distance.

Calling Abby, she explained that she would be gone the next week and asked her to take care of the library. Then she wrote a brief note to Lucas, telling him she was visiting a friend. She wouldn't give him the number or address. She needed total isolation. But she didn't want him to worry, either.

She remade the bed and left the note on her pillow. Then she carried her suitcase down the stairs and out to her car. Frankie wasn't around, so she was able to avoid explaining her behavior to him, too.

So no one told her goodbye, and no one saw her tears.

It was better that way.

Chapter Twelve

Lucas stood over his first wife's grave, traces of his earlier shock on his face.

He hadn't intended to love another woman. Just another woman's child. Beth would understand that. She knew how much he'd wanted their child.

He hoped Beth would understand how things had changed. He'd loved her with the heart of a young man: naive, tender, expecting everything to go right.

But it hadn't.

He was a different man, now. Seasoned with pain and sorrow. And able to love with a maturity and strength he hadn't known he'd had. Had Beth lived, his love for her would've grown to this strength, he was sure.

But she hadn't.

Now he loved Susannah. He'd missed her in his bed, but he'd told himself it was the sex he'd missed. When he'd returned her to his bed, he'd realized, shockingly, that it wasn't the sex, it was the love-making. The holding, the touching, the sharing.

He'd hungered for the sight of her, for the closeness of their togetherness. He'd loved her. Only he hadn't realized it.

When had he begun to love her? From the first, when she intruded into his sad world, refusing to do whatever he asked? When she came to him with her agreement to have his child? Or had it been that first night he'd loved her, when she'd shown him, in spite of her inexperience, how much she needed him, too?

Because she did. He knew, with a joy that grew with each moment, that she loved him as much as he loved her. Susannah, with her generous heart, her determined spirit, wanted him as much as he wanted her.

He walked away from Beth's grave, after bidding her a final goodbye, and headed for the house. The day wasn't over, there was work to be done, but he needed to see Susannah, to hold her, to touch her. To tell her he loved her.

He drove his truck at a breakneck pace, thinking of how he'd left Susannah. She might refuse to let him near her, if he'd read her mood right. But he'd fight for his marriage, for his love, for his heart.

He'd make her listen.

After jerking the truck to a halt, and throwing up pieces of gravel, he sprinted for the house.

"Where's the fire, boss?" Frankie asked as he rushed through the kitchen.

Lucas grinned, the joy spilling out of him. "Gotta find Susannah."

"I think she's gone," Frankie said as he continued rolling out pie dough. "Her car's not here."

Lucas was halfway up the stairs before the man's words penetrated. He tumbled back down the stairs. "What?"

"I said I—"

Lucas ignored him and raced for the window that overlooked where Susannah usually parked her car. "When did she go?"

"I don't know. I came back to the house about half an hour ago to fix lunch and—"

Lucas ignored him and sprinted for the stairs again. He wrenched open the door to Susannah's room and stood on the threshold, studying the neatness. Then he saw the note.

"No, dear God, no," he prayed. God couldn't be so cruel as to give him a second love and then take her away.

But, then, God didn't know how stupid Lucas could be.

The note was simple. She'd gone away to visit a friend. But she'd given no phone number where she could be reached, no address. And she hadn't said when she'd be back. If she'd be back.

He called Abby. "Where's Susannah?"

"Don't you know? She's visiting a friend."

"What friend? Where?"

"I don't know. She hung up before I could ask. What's wrong?" Abby demanded, a growing urgency in her voice.

"She's left me," Lucas whispered, unintentionally

voicing his fears, covering his eyes with his free hand.

"What? What did you do?" Abby asked.

But Lucas couldn't answer. He hung up the phone and sank down to the mattress. What had he done? How could he have been so stupid as to walk away from her without explaining what had happened? He'd thought he'd needed some time.

Now he had more time than he wanted...a lot more time.

Susannah drove into Caliente on Thursday morning.

She'd intended to stay away for a week. But she couldn't. She'd missed the town, her friends, the ranch, Frankie and the cowhands. And Lucas. Dear God, how she'd missed Lucas.

But she punished herself by pulling into a parking space in front of the library. She had abandoned her responsibilities by leaving so suddenly. She needed to see how the library was doing.

Besides, Lucas wasn't expecting her. He probably didn't care when she returned, as long as his baby was well cared for. She might as well practice her resolution to treat him as the father of her child. And nothing else.

She entered the library to find Abby behind the desk.

"Susannah! You're back! Are you all right?" her friend demanded as she rushed around the desk to hug her.

"Yes, of course I'm all right," Susannah replied,

patting Abby's back, wondering what had caused her concern. "I told you I'd be away for a week, but I came back early."

"Does Lucas know?"

"Not yet. He's not expecting me."

"You can say that again," Abby replied.

"Hi, Susannah," Gertie called from across the room. "You're back!"

"Susannah!" Mr. Jones, one of her regular customers, boomed. "'Bout time you came back."

Several other frequent visitors greeted her with the same phrase.

"What's wrong with everyone?" she asked.

"They thought you'd left Lucas," Abby said succinctly.

"Why would they think that? I told you I was going out of town to visit a friend. I left Lucas a note." True, it had been brief, but it was a note.

"You'll have to ask Lucas about that. He pretty much came unglued. The whole town has been worryin' about the two of you. Especially since word got out about you being pregnant." Abby's cheeks actually flushed.

"How did that happen?"

"Well, Lucas and I were talking, and someone overheard. I didn't mean to let it slip, Susannah."

She hugged her friend again. "Don't worry about it. Everyone will know just by looking pretty soon. I'm getting as big as a house." Which would keep Lucas away from her even more, she reminded herself. As if she needed any reminding. She'd spent all the time she was gone preparing herself for his lack of interest. Perhaps even distaste.

"Well, if everything's all right here, I'd better go on to the ranch. I need to unpack and then maybe take a nap. Driving tires me out these days."

"Need me to drive you to the ranch?" Abby asked anxiously.

"Don't be silly. It's not that far. Thank you for taking care of everything here. I'll be in tomorrow."

She turned and headed back for her car.

When she pulled up beside the ranch house a few minutes later, Frankie was already beside the door. He had her suitcase out of the car before she could get out.

"You all right?" he asked, his brow furrowed.

"Of course I am. Did Abby call you?"

"Yeah. We sent for Luke. He'll be here anytime."

Her stomach clutched, and she rubbed it. "There was no need for that. He wasn't even expecting me today."

"Nope. Today's the first time he's given up trying to find you. I don't think he would'a stayed out long, anyway."

Susannah frowned. Trying to find her? She'd left a note. Didn't he read it?

With a shrug, she followed Frankie and her suitcase into the house. He didn't stop until he reached her room, setting the bag down on the floor.

"You hungry? I'll have lunch ready in a few minutes."

"Thanks, Frankie. That would be nice. I'll rest until you call me."

"Want me to call Doc? He could come right out."

"Frankie, I'm fine. Driving tires me out, that's all. I'll rest and then be down for lunch."

He closed the door behind him, and Susannah looked around the neat room. She'd even missed this room. But the one she'd missed most of all was across the hall.

Stop it! You won't be sharing anything in that room anymore.

With a sigh, she sank down onto the bed, slipped off her shoes and put her head on the pillow. She was home.

Lucas was a long way from the barn when one of his cowboys finally caught up with him. He was riding a fence line, doing the most hated work of all, hoping to escape his thoughts. And not having much success.

He saw the rider from a distance, noting his all-out gallop. Uneasiness filled him. Something was wrong. Without hesitation, he urged his horse toward the rider, increasing his speed as he moved.

"Boss, she's back!" the rider gasped as he pulled his horse to a stop.

Lucas's heart leaped. His horse danced, eager to run again, but he paused to ask, "She's okay?"

"Frankie said she's fine."

He didn't ask any more questions. Instead he raced flat out for the house...and his wife.

Sleep had been in short supply this week. Most of the nights he'd paced the floor, worrying, longing for her. Finally, he'd turned to work today, hoping to distract his mind...and she'd come home.

It took almost half an hour to reach the house. News had evidently spread, because several of his cowboys greeted him with broad smiles as he flew from the saddle.

"We'll take care of your horse, boss."

He threw a thanks over his shoulder and ran the rest of the way to the house. She was in the kitchen with Frankie, sitting at the table as if everything were normal. Standing as he entered, she looked apprehensive.

As well she should. She'd scared him to death.

Without speaking, he pulled her to him, wrapping his arms tightly around her. "Don't you ever do that again!" he warned, his voice tight.

"Now, boss, you should talk nice—" Frankie began.

"We're going upstairs," Lucas announced, interrupting his cook's advice.

"But I got lunch almost fixed," Frankie complained.

Susannah had said nothing.

He loosened his grip, staring into her beautiful face. He intended to talk, only talk, but he couldn't help himself as he lowered his mouth to hers. He'd talk in a minute. As soon as he tasted her, made sure she was real and not a figment of his imagination.

He was encouraged as her arms stole around his neck. Then applause and several cheers disrupted the most precious moment in his life to date. Susannah gasped as she looked over his shoulder and saw a number of the staff on the back porch, watching them.

"Shoo, now!" Frankie said, rushing to wave the audience away with a cup towel.

"You, too, Frankie. Go with them," Lucas ordered.

"But, boss, lunch—"

"Turn the stove off and go." His order was stern, and Frankie did as he asked.

When the door closed behind the cook, Susannah looked at him, her eyes wide. "What did you do? Tell everyone we had a fight? The people in town acted as if I'd run away. I—"

"Isn't that what you did?"

She stiffened under his touch, and he knew he'd said the wrong thing. Before he could apologize, she spoke.

"I needed some time away. I didn't mean to worry you." Her voice was solemn, quiet, almost sad.

"Sweetheart, you scared me out of a year's growth."

"The baby is fine. I took good care of it."

"And you? Did you take good care of you?"

"Of course." But her voice was still sad, and she didn't look at him.

"Look, Susannah, when we—the last time—I realized—I loved Beth!" he finally said, unable to figure out exactly how to explain his awakening.

She pulled from his arms and turned her back to him. "Of course. I understand completely."

Instead of turning her, he walked around to face her. "You do?" But the tears streaming down her face told him she didn't. Or she didn't want to hear that he loved her.

She nodded her head.

"Susannah, I want us to have a real marriage. I want—"

He stopped as she turned her back to him again, wiping her tears.

"I can't," she said faintly.

This time he turned her around. "What? Why not? We were getting along just fine. I don't see—"

"I haven't been honest with you."

Her words stopped him cold. What was she talking about? Had she found someone else? Was she going to leave him? His heart ached with fear. "What do you mean?"

"I—I have to tell you something. Then, if you—you still want us to have a real marriage, then—"

"I do!" he insisted, with more fervor than he'd used in his marriage vows. But Susannah meant more to him now.

"I broke our agreement."

"What do you mean? Damn it, Susannah, you're killing me. Tell me what's going on."

She dropped her chin down on her chest, and he leaned closer. "I—I love you."

Her softly whispered words stunned him. Filled him with joy. Worried him. He finally connected them to her earlier explanation that she hadn't been honest.

Lifting her chin, forcing her gaze to his, he said, "Are you telling me you left this week because you love me?"

She nodded.

He closed his eyes and leaned his forehead against hers. "Thank you, God." Then he lowered his head and kissed her. He kissed her to tell her he loved her, to tell her he'd missed her, to tell her he'd never let her go again.

But just in case she didn't understand all those things, he stopped kissing her to tell her in words. He wasn't going to walk away from her again until she understood just how much he loved her.

"Sweetheart, I reacted the way I did last time because I realized I loved you. Completely, totally. More than life itself."

Her tears increased, and she sobbed as she lay her head on his shoulder.

"I promise it's true."

"You…you didn't look like you loved me," she reminded him.

"I was in shock. I'd told myself it was because you were so good in bed that I climbed those stairs earlier and earlier." He tightened his arms around her. "But the truth is, I love you, and I don't ever want you to go away again."

"I don't want to," she assured him, caressing his cheek. "But I was afraid if you saw how much I love you, you'd—you'd want me to go away."

"Never. And I want you in my bed every night, the entire night," he added fiercely. "I hated it when you'd leave me."

"But—"

"I know it's my fault," he admitted, not waiting

for her to speak. "I was an idiot. I was so afraid of being hurt, I was afraid to hold you close."

"I promise I'll try never to hurt you."

He kissed her again.

"I know that, Susannah. And I promise to hold you close forever."

He scooped her into his arms and headed for those stairs that led to heaven. "Mind waiting a little while for lunch?"

She tucked her face into his neck. "I'm more hungry for you than I am for Frankie's cooking."

Satisfaction and eagerness filled him. Susannah was back, to stay, and they'd never be apart again. God had blessed him a second time, and he'd never forget to be grateful.

Epilogue

"**D**amn it, Doc, get in here!" Lucas exploded, entering an emergency room cubicle.

"Settle down, boy. I'll be there as soon as I sew up Jaimie, here." Doc was bent over a three-year-old, with the boy's mother holding him still.

"But Susannah's in pain," Lucas protested. He'd promised himself he'd be calm, but the moment she went into labor, he'd been out of control. He knew it, but he couldn't stop. He was so afraid something would go wrong.

"Nurse Cone will call me if things change. Susannah is going through the normal stages of labor. It's only been a few hours," Doc said calmly, finishing his work. "There now, Jaimie, I suggest you avoid that toy in the future. Okay, young—"

"Doctor, you'd better come," the nurse said from the door, just behind Lucas.

It wasn't a fair contest since he had a head start,

but Lucas beat Doc to Susannah's side by a long shot. "Sweetheart, are you all right?"

Susannah, in the throes of another pain, couldn't answer at once. It was the nurse's calm voice that reassured him. "Of course she is. But I don't think it will be much longer."

Doc settled at the end of the table and examined Susannah. "You're faster than I thought, young lady. Or maybe this baby is impatient, like his daddy."

Susannah drew a deep breath and smiled. Lucas kissed her forehead, then stroked her cheek. "Hold on, sweetheart. Doc's going to take care of everything."

"Don't you believe him for a minute," Doc contradicted. "I'm just along for the ride. You and Junior here are the ones doing all the work. It's time now. I want you to push," he urged.

Susannah, clutching Lucas's hand, followed directions. Only a few minutes later, Doc held the next generation of Boyd men in his hands.

"He's a fine, healthy boy, Susannah," Doc assured her.

Lucas glanced at his son, but his attention was focused on his wife. "Are you okay, sweetheart? Can I get you anything? Does it hurt?"

"You can bring our son here," she said. When her baby was laid in her arms, Susannah beamed at her husband. "See, I told you everything would be fine."

His hand trembling, Lucas touched first his child and then his wife's face. "Yes, you did. And you were right, as always. I love you."

He gently kissed her soft lips.

"So next time I can have a daughter?" she teased.

They'd had several arguments over the topic of more children. Susannah wanted them, but Lucas wasn't sure he could risk losing her again. She'd made him promise to change his mind if she came through this delivery without difficulties.

"We'll see. Doc can—"

"Lucas, you promised," she reminded him, cuddling her infant against her. "Besides, we make beautiful babies together. How could you say no?"

He stared at his beloved wife and child and only shook his head. He'd been truly blessed when Susannah came into his life. He never wanted to chance losing her.

But he also knew he could never deny her anything. And he suspected he'd have difficulty doing that with his children, too. His son grabbed hold of his finger, trying to carry this new object to his mouth.

Lucas tucked Susannah's head against his shoulder. "I suppose we could consider a little girl. In a year or two. If you're sure."

Smiling at him, her love filling her eyes, Susannah nodded her head. "Yes, in a year or two."

"But only if you promise she'll look just like you," he added.

"Okay, but only if *you* promise you'll love me when I'm fat and lumpy again."

She'd worried about losing her figure, but Lucas had delighted in every change, holding her close each night, giving thanks for her.

"Done," he agreed, with no hesitation at all. And with another loving smile, he kissed her again, a kiss that communicated all the husbandly devotion that swelled his heart.

* * * * *

Silhouette Romance
celebrates the joys
of first love in
VIRGIN BRIDES

September 1998:
THE GUARDIAN'S BRIDE
by Laurie Paige (#1318)
A young heiress, desperately in love with her
older, wealthy guardian, dreams of wedding the
tender tycoon. But he has plans to marry
her off to another....

October 1998:
THE NINE-MONTH BRIDE
by Judy Christenberry (#1324)
A widowed rancher who wants an heir and a prim librarian
who wants a baby decide to marry for convenience—but will
motherhood make this man and wife rethink their
temporary vows?

November 1998:
A BRIDE TO HONOR by Arlene James (#1330)
A pretty party planner falls for a charming, honor-bound
millionaire who's being roped into a loveless marriage. When
the wedding day arrives, will *she* be his blushing bride?

December 1998:
A KISS, A KID AND A MISTLETOE BRIDE (#1336)
When a scandalous single dad returns home at
Christmas, he encounters the golden girl he'd fallen
for one magical night a lifetime before.

Available at your favorite retail outlet.

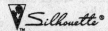

Take 2 bestselling love stories FREE

Plus get a FREE surprise gift!

Special Limited-Time Offer

Mail to Silhouette Reader Service™

> 3010 Walden Avenue
> P.O. Box 1867
> Buffalo, N.Y. 14240-1867

YES! Please send me 2 free Silhouette Romance™ novels and my free surprise gift. Then send me 6 brand-new novels every month, which I will receive months before they appear in bookstores. Bill me at the low price of $2.90 each plus 25¢ delivery and applicable sales tax, if any.* That's the complete price, and a saving of over 10% off the cover prices—quite a bargain! I understand that accepting the books and gift places me under no obligation ever to buy any books. I can always return a shipment and cancel at any time. Even if I never buy another book from Silhouette, the 2 free books and the surprise gift are mine to keep forever.

215 SEN CH7S

Name	(PLEASE PRINT)	
Address	Apt. No.	
City	State	Zip

This offer is limited to one order per household and not valid to present Silhouette Romance™ subscribers. *Terms and prices are subject to change without notice. Sales tax applicable in N.Y.

USROM-98   ©1990 Harlequin Enterprises Limited

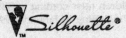

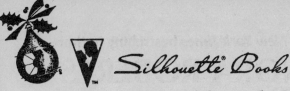
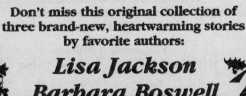

FOLLOW THAT BABY...

the fabulous cross-line series featuring the infamously wealthy Wentworth family...continues with:

THE DADDY AND
THE BABY DOCTOR

by **Kristin Morgan**

(Romance, 11/98)

The search for the mysterious Sabrina Jensen pits a seasoned soldier—and single dad—against a tempting baby doctor who knows Sabrina's best-kept secret....

Available at your favorite retail outlet, only from

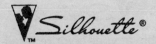

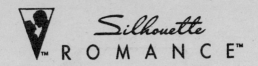

Silhouette ROMANCE™

COMING NEXT MONTH